The Land's Lord

The Land's Lord

T. OBINKARAM ECHEWA

LAWRENCE HILL & COMPANY

Westport, Connecticut

Library of Congress Cataloging in Publication Data
Echewa, T.   Obinkaram.
The land's Lord.
I.   Title
PZ4.E18Lan3   (PR9387.9E27)   823   76-18327
ISBN 0-88208-069-5
ISBN 0-88208-070-9 pbk.

First published in Great Britain in 1976 by
Heinemann Educational Books Ltd.

Library of Congress Catalog Card Number: LC: 76-18327
ISBN: 0-88208-069-5 (cloth edition)
ISBN: 0-88208-070-9 (paperback edition)

First U.S. Edition, September, 1976

1   2   3   4   5   6   7   8   9   10

Lawrence Hill & Company, Publishers, Inc.

Manufactured in the United States of America
by Ray Freiman & Company

To my Father
for His Faith

1

Libera nos, Domine!

He walked as if he had to get somewhere at an appointed time. His legs kicked noisily into the large folds of his soutane. And then he stopped. The mission was ahead. The village was behind. He looked in one direction and then the other, uncertain which way salvation lay. He opened his breviary as if the answer could be found there.

Do me justice, Oh God, and fight my fight against a faithless people. For you, Oh God, are my strength: why do you keep me so far away; why must I go about in mourning with the enemy oppressing me?

He snapped the book shut and walked forward again. God had not chosen to answer.

'All gods are a little mad', old man Ahamba had often remarked to him, his strong jaws and bad teeth bearing heavily on a kola nut. 'If you have a mind to serve them properly, you should be a little drunk yourself.'

Were they also a little deaf?

The sun was falling; the shadows were lengthening. The forest sat there as ever on either side of him, riotously green and festering with shadows and mysteries the sun never penetrated. Animals tame and wild headed home from the day's foraging. In the village hut complexes just behind him, there were the measured tones of pestles pounding on the contents of hollow mortars. Supper smoke rose out of numerous kitchens and curled skywards like so many sacrifices to the pagan gods.

Then there was his mission, a spot of enforced baldness, a tonsure on the green jungle, which was kept at bay temporarily by a fence. But the jungle loathed any breaches of its dominion, and never relented in its efforts to digest, absorb and re-integrate everything into itself. Dried fence posts were quickly consumed by hordes of white termites. Others sprouted and grew into luxuriant bushes, and soon became part of what they were supposed to keep in check. Seeded bird droppings germinated on the thatch roof of the rectory. Where Philip's kitchen and woodshed leaked, weeds exploded out of the damp floor.

1

He took a cursory look at the brown and obtuse-angled thatch of the old church, then a much longer look at the low but expansive perimeter of the new church. Solid. Redoubtable. Earthbound! At the far end of the clearing was his rectory. A tall man would have to bend to get under the eaves which hung over the rectory's veranda – they were so low. But he did not have to bend, being an inch or more shorter than five and half feet. 'Fada Nwambee', his parishioners had called him when they first saw him. 'The Orphan Priest'. He had looked like an orphan to them, underfed and ill-used.

Ill-used by circumstances. Undernourished by God's actual grace.

He shrugged and continued walking, feeling a little of the confidence of his priestly call. His voluminous white soutane gave him bulk. His large flowing beard conferred substance. In the year he had already spent here, the sun had browned away the milky transparency of his skin.

His servant and cook, Philip, appeared on the veranda of the rectory, waving. Supper was probably ready, he thought, but he did not acknowledge Philip's gesture. He kept walking, past the mission, unable or uninclined to will himself to stop.

About half a mile past the mission he entered a bush trail heading west towards the falling sun, wondering a little, but only a little, where the trail led, or why anyone would want to walk it, for there seemed to be nothing in that direction except the green forest stretching endlessly. The bushes parted unwillingly to let him pass. Thorny shrubs and sharp blades of andropogon and elephant grass barred his way, but he urged them aside with firm hands, and walked unflinchingly, squinting occasionally from the glare of the sun in his face.

Then from the distance his ears picked up the faint echoes of new wailing at Paul's house. At first the cries merely brushed against his hearing, but then they mixed with his thoughts and rose to an intensity that made him wince. The whole forest seemed to reverberate with them. Musty thoughts disinterred from their places of hiding in the remotest recesses of his mind, secret fears and abandoned hopes, unanswerable questions about life and death and God – they all grappled with one another and stampeded like giddy monsters across the landscape of his mind. Martha, the widow of Paul who had just died. An oiled corpse with a rosary and a cross of raffia pith in its hands. Martha's spasmodic flailings and body contortions, the paroxysms of grief which seized her and shook her violently. She thrashed about like a beheaded snake, wriggling and throwing herself on the ground over and over. His parishioners praying

2

the rosary, reciting the Litany of the Blessed Virgin for some reason in English.

Amiss on-us!
Amiss on-us!
Fray-frus!
Fray-frus!

Ostensibly God who understood everything understood that they meant to say 'Have mercy on us!' and 'Pray for us!' He understood their intentions.

But why are we not redeemed by our best intentions?

Some of the men tried to restrain Martha, to keep her from injuring herself. But she kept screaming: 'Why? God, why?' Her cries resonated in his ears.

Why?

God did not answer. God did not feel obliged to answer. But Martha had dared to ask. His parishioners, all the people of the village, had the temerity he lacked. They queried their gods and insisted on answers.

Old man Ahamba: What use is a god is you cannot expect anything of him?

'No, no', Father Higler objected, and then answered in the translation of a German proverb. A god that can be understood is no god.

But would more understanding diminish God's godliness?

He fought frantically with a spider web that had netted his face – punching, spitting, flailing, feeling himself snared in the entangling meshes under the claws of the horrible creature. He broke into a run to escape its clutches, stopped briefly when his glasses fell from his face, brushed off the lenses on his belly and walked forward again, urged on by a force he could not understand. His approach unsettled numerous denizens of the forest and sent them scurrying noisily but invisibly into the undergrowth. Flies and beetles buzzed his ears and slammed into his face. Twigs snapped under his feet.

The trail opened into a small yam and cassava farm from which the yams had been dug up, leaving little mounds and holes, heaps of twigs and dried twiners. Stalks of unharvested cassava rose out of the rich alluvium; the winds heaved their palmate leaves and wafted a stench across his nostrils.

He looked up at the infinite and iridescent sky, streaked with gold and purple, flaring into red in the low horizon just above the green tree tops where the sun had fallen. There was quiet here but not peace. The mind exploded in riot, trying to wrestle free of turbulent echoes, from the encroaching darkness. The light was surrendering to darkness.

And the light shineth in the darkness?
And the darkness apprehendeth it not?

God who created the world – could He not bear to look at it all at once? Is that why He chose to light only half of it at one time? The sky was no nearer here than in England or Alsace. Salvation was no nearer, fate no more amenable to persuasion. There were no bargain tickets to heaven, no packaged formulas of plenary indulgences.

He turned, following the effluvium that wafted across his nostrils and walked to a low, thick bush.

Flies.

Some sat on leaves, taxiing up and down and beating their wings. Others circled. He circled himself to the far side of the bush. A multitude of them rose in a tumultuous and discordant chorus, bombed his face, swirled around him. And then he beheld for the first time, the object of their assembly, the carcass of a sacrificial dog, rotting on a make-shift shrine. Two Y-shaped boughs driven into the earth were bridged by a straight pole, and on the latter the dog's legs were trussed, making him appear to have been caught in the middle of a somersaulting trick. Head hanging back, teeth bared in an ugly and defiant snarl, tongue dangling on one side in the final act of defiance. Blue-glass eyeballs lost in eternal reverie. Earholes plugged with crawling flies. Various other objects lay around the altar – egg shells, manilas and cowries, two decorated gourds that might have held some food earlier.

Hands folded across his chest, Father Higler stood staring at these tributes to an unknown idol, evidences of human hope and fear, and ultimately, he felt, folly. Who had sacrificed these things to what god? And with what profit? He focused on each object in turn, wondering what part it had played in the ritual.

Forgive them, O Lord, for they know not what they do!

And then he whirled around. A mephistophelian presence had been hovering just behind his shoulder, an incubus born of his fears. But he saw nothing, save the blue-tinted evening mist which was just beginning to float over the forest, and the heraldic darkness beginning to weave the vegetation together in the deeper recesses of the forest. He scoured the surroundings with his eyes, and once again wondered why anybody from the village would come this far to make a farm. There was plenty of farming land much nearer the village. But the place and its inhabitants subscribed to a different order of logic. They never tried to push the jungle back, but rather found little places for themselves within it. They

4

had it around them breathing its noxious odours, pulsing and churning with malaria and yellow fever. Every native foot, it seemed, gladly, or at least, resignedly, played host to a colony of chiggers. The ringworm ran happy circles on the heads of the children. Roaches, lizards, geckos in their houses did not seem to bother them. They seemed innured to even the flies and the mosquitoes – all of them made of the same primordial stuff – the people, the forest, and the other denizens of the forest – unfinished, unrefined and unreconstituted nature. Where they farmed or otherwise violated the forest, they did so with a deference and respect, on a small spot like this one and for a short lease only. And after they had harvested their crops, the forest moved back quickly to reclaim its territory.

Kpoi! Kpoi! Kpoi!

The measured tones of the *ekwe*, the sonorous hollowed log that now served him as church bell. God, would his bell ever arrive from England? Would he ever be able to set this forest trembling with its tintinnabulations? – That was Philip sounding the angelus. He crossed himself. 'The angel of the Lord declared unto Mary. And she was conceived of the Holy Ghost . . .'

'She was?' old Ahamba said, breaking into a bad-toothed cackle. 'Akhee! khee-khee . . . I say your gods are strange, White Man. And quite adventuresome. Yes, they are. Akhee! khee-khee . . .'

All of a sudden he noticed the darkness had almost completely comprehended the light, and he hastened towards the mouth of the path which had brought him there. He walked fast, no longer using his hands to urge the branches aside, but thrusting himself into them. Shortly after, he broke into a trot, then to a run, then a dead run. The commotion of his hasty passage commingled with his fears and resonated in his imagination to hundreds of howling, drunken demons. Branches slapped his chest and face, clawed at his soutane and ripped off large kerchiefs from it. He fell, rose, fell again, rose again like a proverbial just man, and he ran still faster, a million legionnaire devils at his heels.

Where the trail opened onto the road he ran into someone, and they both fell down.

'Jesus Christ in heaven!'

'Fada!'

'Philip! My God!' He huffed and did not attempt to rise.

'Fada, what happen?' Philip offered a sturdy black hand. He took it and hoisted himself up.

'I'm all right, Philip.' He glanced back whence he had come, as if to be sure, then reached into the pocket of what was left of his soutane, took out his glasses and put them on.

'Fada, there is blood on your hand.'

'Yes, yes, Philip.' He looked at the hand and wiped it off behind his back. 'Just scratches. I must have hundreds of them. All over . . .'

'And your soutane. It is torn in one hundred places. Look, look all over.'

'Yes, Philip. My best soutane too. How did you get here? Were you trailing me?'

'Fada, I see you pass the mission, and I begin to wonder. So I come. When I get here and see you enter the bush, I decide to wait.'

'H'm . . .'

'Fada, your one shoe. You are naked on one foot.'

'Yes, Philip.' He looked at the mouth of the trail. 'Maybe in the morning you can go and look for it. After mass.'

'Fada, I go now to find it.' He walked off into the trail.

'No need to go now,' Father Higler protested. 'It's too dark already.'

But Philip was on his way. He turned to acknowledge Father Higler's protest but did not break his stride. The darkening forest quickly swallowed him.

Father Higler removed his other shoe and limped bare-footed back to his mission. He sat on the veranda of the rectory in his sweaty socks; the irreparable remains of his soutane dangled over the half wall. His eyes roamed without focus over the darkening space of the mission. The ritual enactment of another day's passage. Another day. One day added itself to another in quick succession – inexorably. He had been here for a year now. What good works, what indulgences had he entered in his account today?

He exhaled heavily, opened his breviary to read a little more of his daily office. But his attention strayed, his body smarted from what seemed like dozens of bruises and pin pricks. Life here was immediate, earthly and *real*, and seemed to abhor abstractions like the Latin phrases of his breviary, which he had already memorized from years of repetition. And his most ardent prayers – could they raise by one inch the wall of his new and earth-bound church? No power available to him, no graces he could draw upon or even dare to hope for could diminish the sinister majesty that stood guard around his tiny clearing.

Unless the Lord builds the city, they labour in vain that try to build it!

But he had come here to do not to think, to work not to pray, for in some fifteen years as a contemplative he had served an abstract God,

6

sublimate and rarefied beyond all understanding, had pursued him zealously with a pious faith and an enthusiastic imagination. Calloused knees. Dreamy eyes. The twilight of claustrophobic chapels, panelled in heavy oak and haunted by saintly ghosts. Faith supported on a cloud of prayers.

Philip returned, shoe in one hand, a bunch of rags shredded from the priest's soutane in the other. The servant laid the shoe at the master's foot, picked up the remnants of the soutane and spread them out, holding the tips of the sleeves as if he were measuring the garment on himself. He then looked at the ball of rags he had brought back, shook his head and rolled everything into one big ball.

'Fada eat first or baff first?'

'Bath.'

'Yes, Fada.'

'Boil the water, Philip.'

'Fada, I already boil.'

'Okay. Pour it in the wash basin then. What's for night chop?'

'The remainder of the fowl meat Fada did not finish yesterday.'

'H'm. Okay. Call me when you have poured the water.'

The space before him darkened further. Darkness seemed to ooze from the sky, the ground and circumscribing forest. He thought of God somewhere out or up there stage-managing this final phase of the transition, ordering that the light on his stage be dimmed, and put out.

You made the moon to mark the seasons;
The sun knows the hour of its setting.
You bring darkness and it is night
Then all the beasts of the forest roam about.

Philip summoned him to his bath. He tested the water with his fingers and then stepped into the tin tub. Lowered himself gingerly into the water. At first it felt abrasive and stinging on his scratches, but at length it felt soothing and refreshing like a pool of divine grace. He soaped and scrubbed himself slowly, and by repeated acts of the will kept his mind free of all thought. He had nowhere else to go but bed. Another day. Life here was sometimes painfully slow. At other times it was giddy and spasmodic. The earth seemed to rotate unevenly, starting with a quick jerk early in the morning, the crystal and opalescent morning vanishing before you even noticed it, and then the afternoon coming in with its heat and settling. The good was transient, the bad lingering. And then evening. Twilight was less than a blink; night came in a hurry, rapidly besmudging the atmosphere.

He heard Philip washing the hurricane lamp, then a new burst of wailing from the direction of Paul's house. He had a Requiem Mass to say in the morning. Paul did not have to die now. A proverb someone had uttered that afternoon idled into his mind. 'A guest at a funeral does not moan louder than those who are bereaved.' God was the owner of this vineyard. He was only a labourer in it, a mere hireling.

'Philip!'

'Fada.'

'Let me have some tea with supper.'

'Yes Fada.'

Yes Fada. Yes Fada. Yes Fada. Philip rarely said anything else but Yes Fada. He imagined a conversation with the servant.

'Look, Philip, you have a soul.'

'Yes Fada.'

'And you have to save this soul.'

'Yes Fada.'

'And here's what you have to do to save your soul.'

'Yes Fada.'

What was Philip's quest? What did he want from God and his Holy Church?

Faith.

Salvation.

That was what he and all the other parishioners had answered at their baptism.

Old man Ahamba: 'Akhee! Khee-khee! I tell you, White Man, we already have gods here that do nothing for us but are hungry for our sacrifices. What we need is a god who does something for us. Akhee! Akhee-khee! . . .'

Philip hung a lamp by the door of the bath shed.

Father Higler towelled himself. Back in the hut-rectory he donned a pair of khaki shorts and a white shirt. Then he ate. Philip watched his dinner activities from the kitchen door. He had a nature which seemed capable of finding fulfilment in simply watching another man eat. As soon as he was done, Philip rushed up with the tea kettle.

The pouring ceremonies over, the servant took the plates away to the kitchen. Washed. Cleaned. Locked the door. Then he came to where Father Higler sat, thoughtfully soaking his moustache in hot tea.

'Fada want anything more?'

'No, Philip.'

'I can go now?'

'Yes, Philip.'
'Yes Fada. Goodnight Fada.'
'Goodnight.'

Philip stepped into the darkness, and the darkness swallowed him.

For Father Higler, the quiet crept closer, and the loneliness deepened. The darkness, now solid, stood just a few feet away beyond the circle of light shed by the hurricane lamp. The moon was out of phase; there was no traffic on the road. The villagers retired early – day, they felt, and not night, was given to them to roam. He dozed.

Incline unto my aid, Oh God!
O Lord, make haste to help me!

For here he was, a small, bearded Alsatian, trying to impose his will on this primeval land and tame it, to push the jungle back and light the darkness. He was the only European within thirty miles. A conquering army of one. He had recruited some local help, but the first lieutenant was due a burial in the morning.

'Come to me all ye who labour and are burdened, and I will refresh you!'

They had come, those of them in greatest distress, those who had despaired of other sources of succour. They listened attentively to his sermons, held on to his promises like certificates of indebtedness – to be cashed in when the need arose. And they wanted their relief here, not in heaven. Heaven could come later as their crowning bonus. The village yielded its people grudgingly, and yielded only the least blessed among them.

Old man Ahamba: Yes, White Man, if your god can work a miracle on all these people you now have, I tell you something, I will throw away my idols and join your church myself!

Would he be a hero here and have his name marked with stars in the book of life? Or would this churning jungle, this White Man's Grave swallow him, all his efforts, all his hopes. What power of alchemy, what flash flood of God's sanctifying grace would turn him, a cowardly soldier who had once fled from battle, into a heroic priest?

Undistinguished life. Undistinguished death. Uncertain salvation.

Sleep weighed heavily on his eyes. He ambled to the chapel and prayed for the cardinal virtues of faith, hope and charity: Lord, I love you. Help me to love you more and my fellow men because of you. Lord, secure and anchor my hope in you for I am always driven between presumption and despair. Lord, I believe in you. Help my unbelief. And then his mind balked, shied like a horse before the fearful thing. But he spurred himself on, and with an effort he finally managed to say it. Lord, please believe in me too! He then rose to pour some kerosene in the sanctuary lamp, dozed for a few more moments in lieu of further meditation, then locked the doors and went to his bedroom.

Sleep came quickly, but in those hesitant moments when the spirit of consciousness was taking leave of his senses, the spectre of the sacrificial dog wafted eerily into his mind. He fought to erase it, and to shake himself into wakefulness. However, he felt himself trapped by waves and waves of swirling darkness. Pithy darkness. Putrid mire. Wild, luxuriant ferns grew out of his mouth and nostrils, sinking their roots into his entrails, drawing the blood and the life juices out of him, digesting him. He awakened shaken.

'God!'

From all ill dreams defend our eyes
From nightly fears and fantasies.
You who dwell in the shelter of the Most High
You will not fear the terror of the night
Nor the plague that prowls in darkness.

Christe, audi nos!

2

'This is like a grave you are digging for your enemy,' Genesis said. 'So deep that if he wakes from death he cannot climb out of it.'

'Dig,' John retorted. 'Dig, my man, before they come upon us with the corpse. You have rested enough.'

'Rest? Me, rest? I have not known any rest since my mother delivered me.'

'Dig!'

Thuds of blunt metal hoes stabbing the soft belly of the land. The grave has already swallowed John, the shorter man, and has Genesis more than neck-deep. A ridge of loose earth lines its lips. The men spit, huff and curse when from time to time chunks of red, damp, sub-soil roll off the ridge back on them. The truncated calabash which they use to transport the earth makes frequent trips from the bottom to the top. And then back again.

'I say this is deep enough,' Genesis said.

'Fada said dig until when you raise your hand the fingers do not show out.'

'Me or you to raise hands?'

'You.'

'I do not know why it has to be so deep. After all, it is a grave for one person, and they are not going to stand up the coffin.'

'If it had not been for those roots near the top . . . We are lucky it is not a very hot day today.'

'Hot enough.'

Each had his own hoe, but they shared the calabash. They dug for a while in silence which was total except for the thuds of their hoes against the red bosom of the earth. A sunless, cheerless atmosphere hung above them. It was that time of day between midmorning and noon when all aspects of the new day simultaneously seemed to lose their enthusiasms. The birds had fed and sung themselves to drowsiness. People in the farms had hoed away their early energies. Sheep and goats lay under the trees rehashing what they had gorged for breakfast. The grasshoppers snapped lazily, and faint breezes blew just hard enough to tickle the sweat on a man's face, and to make the leaves shake a little, just a little, as if afraid to wake something asleep.

Four hoefuls filled the calabash. One of the two men threw it out, while the other dug up another hoeful and waited for the calabash to return. The one who threw in the first hoeful got to throw out the calabash. That way, they alternated.

'I do not know why he chose me as one of those to cut down the bush for this burying ground, and then to dig this grave,' Genesis said.

'He likes you,' John replied.

'That is not a way I like to be liked. And his liking has not helped me too much in the past. I am still where I am, and at a time like this when death is sniffing about it is best to keep your head low, and not stand out.'

'Death will find you if he is looking for you. You know what they say about a man's fate being like his heel and following him everywhere. Still, I agree with you somewhat. I do not think it is good to clear up a place and call it a burying ground. And have it standing there waiting. That is like inviting death.'

'Like making a coffin and then waiting for a corpse to put in it.'

'Or like digging a grave and leaving it empty in case someone dies.'

Genesis, smiling, 'You know the saying that the villagers should never hear the coffin maker praying to the gods to give him more business. Especially those with sick relatives.'

'You are afraid of death, I see?'

'You are not?'

'But there is reward in heaven, is there not?' John said, and Genesis could not quite determine how serious he was. 'A place of rest and well being. Away from these sweats and tears. Is that not what Fada says?'

'When you get there. And if you get there, because you remember he says not everybody will get there. Me, I want to go there, but I am not ready to go now-now.'

John laughed. 'You think Paul has gone to heaven?'

'I do not know. Did Fada not hear his confession and give him Last Sacrament?'

'He did. Still you keep hearing things. His death was strange. You think it was just ordinary death? And nothing behind it?'

'No death is ordinary. But what was there behind that of Paul? What have you heard?'

'There was his father whom he never buried fully according to custom. No second burial ceremony. Then they say the jujus were angry. When he fell sick I heard somebody went to consult a seer on his behalf. Then a famous medicine man came from out of town to close the eyes of the jujus. They kept it very secret because they did not want Fada to hear.'

To close the eye of a juju –
Prepare your medicine and make it strong.

Catch a large male lizard – oketikpo – the one with the red crown, that sits atop the roofs at noon time nodding assent to all the children's questions.

Summon the recalcitrant god with the correct incantations.

Invoke his name over the lizard.

Juo ya ogu muo na madu! (Impeach him on the binding logic of the relationship between gods and men!)

For when gods get due sacrifice men should get their just desserts.

Dignum et justum est.

The right hand must wash the left hand, just as the left hand must wash the right hand.

Equum et salutare.

No – It may be fitting and just, but hardly conducive to salvation to insist that the gods do their part.

You boldly recount the god's offenses.

Should the gods be allowed to flout common sense or to exempt themselves from reason?

So you read the reproaches:

My god, what have I done to you? In what way have I grieved you? Answer me! What more ought I to do for you that I have not already done?

The god is speechless.

Make your medicine into a paste and stuff the lizard full of it. Knead it over his eyes that he may not see, his ears that he may not hear, his mouth that he may not curse you.

Then let the lizard go.

And that should be one god put to silence!

'And still he died,' Genesis said. 'The medicine was no help. And the Mass Fada said for him.'

'Nothing is much good,' John replied.

'But I will stay with the church,' Genesis said. 'I will keep on going to confession and communion.'

John looked at Genesis, a little surprised by his act of faith.

'For another four or five months,' Genesis continued. 'My wife is now pregnant.'

'Ah, really! Little wonder then.'

'I must wait and see what she delivers.'

Genesis wanted a son. Even on the day Father Schlotz, Father Higler's predecessor who opened the mission, baptized him, begetting a son rather than eternal salvation had been foremost on Genesis' mind.

Father Schlotz had asked, 'What do you desire from the church of God?'

'A son.'

Clearly an unacceptable response. He should have desired faith, a staunch faith which would guide him to life everlasting. And perhaps as a result of that pusillanimity God had answered Genesis' prayers in half measure only. His wife, until then fruitless, had conceived and in due time delivered a healthy bouncy baby girl. A girl is better than nothing, and so Genesis had grunted and swallowed and named her Iheariochi – What

Was Requested of God (?) — and decided to give God another chance, believing as much as he could, praying as hard as he could.

'I stay on,' John said, 'because there is nowhere else to go. And the church is cheaper than the jujus. And since I am now usher, nobody can notice what I do not put into the plate on Sunday. And this is the first time I was ever appointed anything.'

'We all have our reasons,' Genesis replied. 'I think we now have enough grave.'

John raised his right hand for a measurement. 'Give it the length of one hoe, while I go out and find an egg and a piece of Efanim rock. You know we cannot leave this grave without leaving it something in exchange for our heads. Help me out.'

John dug his toes into the wall of the grave and attempted to scramble out with Genesis pushing at his buttocks. But he could not secure a handhold and his efforts brought down avalanches of loose earth on both of them. Finally Genesis stooped, John climbed on his shoulders, Genesis stood, and John was able to get out. He made the Sign of the Cross on himself and cast his gaze about.

Genesis asked, 'Can you tell how far the mass has gone?'

John looked towards the church building. A song swelled from there, as if in answer:

Now the books are open spread
Now the writing must be read
Which condemns the quick and dead.

John clapped his hands free of soil and began walking towards the village.

Within the church itself, to the congregation that had come to bury Paul, Father Higler was raising a sermon to a height of fervence and eloquence unusual for him, using the flames of hell to fire the base metal of their hearts and threats of God's vindictive wrath to bend their minds towards salvation.

'It could have been you,' he was saying, 'lying now in that coffin!' He gestured frenziedly, like a symphony conductor gone berserk, jabbed and flailed his hands at their refractoriness. 'You! No, not the person next to you! You!' The veins in his face flicked and vibed like plucked strings. 'Satan tries to make you believe it will always be somebody else, but some day it will be you. You! The question is: When that undeniable call comes, will you be ready? Are you ready now? . . . The coffin here before us should be a lesson to all. We all saw Paul last Sunday as he came to receive Holy Communion, and as he made the announcements after mass. How many of you knew then that that was the last time he would be walking up to this altar on his own power? Some of you saw him even later. His wife was talking to him when the Lord issued the awesome call.

'The holy gospels have warned us to be constantly on the watch for we know not the day nor the hour of the Lord's coming. "Delay not in being converted unto the Lord," we have been told, "and defer not from day to day. For the wrath of the Lord will come in a sudden. And in his vengeance he will destroy thee." '

He paused, looked at the coffin which bridged the space between two low stools – roughly planed iroko wood, entirely without decoration. At the end nearer him a nail had missed its mark and torn through the skin of the wood. He pulled a handkerchief from inside the sleeve of his tunic, wiped his nostril, and stuffed the scarf back into his sleeve. Then he resumed preaching.

He was suffused with an exhilarating sensation, a warm glow of exultation like a stage performer whose senses tingle with orgasmic reverberations from the applauses of an appreciative audience. He felt he was reaching them, perhaps not with a momentous impact, but with some impact nonetheless. He was tugging at their hearts; he could see their faces serious and drawn, their eyes fixed on him rather than wandering among the rest of the congregation. There was little shifting in the seats and no shuffling of feet.

He was not deceived, though, about what he had awakened in them. Fear. But fear was fair enough. As a start. Was the fear of the Lord not the beginning of all wisdom? Piety? Salvation?

'But your god is a stranger here,' Old Man Ahamba would say. 'Like you. He does not know us and our ways. How can he provide our needs? Do not the gods, like men, have their own territories? Your god, he does not even live here. He is not a native of our soil, our skies or our forests.'

Father Higler would reply, 'He most certainly is.'

'He is? He is here among us?'

'Yes. The almighty and eternal God is everywhere.'

'He cannot be. Even the land is divided by rivers and seas. The very sky has limits, and boundaries, and when it is raining in one place, it may be shining in another.'

'True, but God who made the universe, the earth and the sky, rain and sunshine – everything – knows no limitations. He is in all of his creation. Everywhere!'

'And you did not bring him with you? It was not you who brought him here?'

'No! He needs no bringing anywhere. He was always here. Always will be.'

'Even before you came he was here?'

'Yes, even before I came. From all eternity he has been among you.'

'Then why did you come?'

He had no answer. He swallowed once, twice. The question was subversive; it sought to make his coming redundant. The answers he attempted gummed in his throat like morsels of plaster. 'To tell you about him,' he finally said. 'To help you discover him, even if he was here all the time.'

'He, this god of yours, was among us since time began, and we did not know? I find that strange, White Man. Strange. But life is full of strangeness. So all I can say is: Let him prove himself. If he can absorb the thunderbolt of our Amadioha or make more powerful ones, then I say he is to be feared.'

Fear. Fear of death. Fear of the uncertainty which lies beyond death.

Faith. Faith, oh God, grant them your gift of faith!

But God vouchsafed no signs to encourage faith. The faithful and the faithless were indiscriminately condemned to wayward suffering and haphazard death. No signs, no haloes, marked the true believers. Nothing exempted them from the common lot.

So, as was often the case with Father Higler, a touch of despair crept over the edges of his mild exultation, as he continued to paint desperate pictures of worms that never died and fires that never quenched and invited his hearers to imagine how long it would take to empty out the mighty Imo River of all its waters, in all its length and breadth, using only a tiny coconut shell. That, he said, was but one moment, one twinkling, in the eye of eternity. What, if not death or the fear of eternal damnation could shake them out of apathy? They sat before him in their sodality, a crowd of torpid eyes in a sea of dark faces, bound together in their obduracy. It was as if they had been converted against their will and had since resigned the power to will anything. 'It is you who wants us saved,' they seemed to be saying. 'You save us!'

And thus it seemed that his own eternal fate had become inextricably mingled with theirs, and he could save himself only by saving them. In a monastery, the link with God was direct through prayer; there were no measures of success, only of constancy and fervence, and with practice the contemplative eye turned the dim mirror of faith into a burning lens and fired the imagination to a dazzling incandescence. But here they were the mediators of his efforts, arbiters of his success, witnesses to his failure –

a saturnine jury between him and God – and he could not be sure whether to blame his own shortcomings or their obstinacy for their lack of zeal.

He fingered his beard one last time, drawing it between his fingers and his thumb from the jaw to his tip. Then he wiped his non-existent forelock and uttered a final warning from the gospels. 'What I say to you I say to all: Watch!'

His hand navigated through his vestments into the pocket of his soutane and from thence he pulled out a piece of paper, glanced at it and said: 'The bricklayers did not work yesterday because nobody brought them water. Those of you who were supposed to fetch them water for this week must do so tomorrow and on Friday. Let me repeat that: Those of you . . .' He then turned around and intoned in Latin: *'Credo in unum Deum . . .'*

Mumble, mumble, mumble, which God understood but the congregation did not. There were those among them, in fact, who maintained that God understood only Latin and English, especially Latin. That was why the priest always prayed in Latin and why their own prayers often went nowhere and brought no results. God, like the priest, had his difficulties with Igbo.

A drab November day, one of those just before the harmattan when the skies fake a threat of rain but everyone knows it is only a fake. A morbid atmosphere suffused by the aura of uncertainty. In the oil bean trees, the swallows have recently returned from their sojourn up north where they weathered the rains. They stretch their wings and whistle occasional alarms. The golden aspilia feature small terminal inflorescences. The andropogon has lost its intense greenness, and the blades are thrashing about in unreconciled rhythms.

On the north corner of the mission – Saint Peter Claver's – named after the Caribbean slave priest, a fresh grave is waiting to receive its man. Father Higler is consecrating it and the new grave yard cleaned the day before as a resting place for all the mission's faithful, banishing the devil and his cohorts from hence, conjuring the holy angels to stand watch, imploring God to receive the soul of the faithful servant, Paul, to close his eyes to sins occasioned by human fraility, to forget his justice and remember his mercy.

For if you, O Lord, mark iniquities, Lord, who can stand?

17

The drone and undulating hum of Latin phrases. The congregation waits with patience and attention for the pauses so they can come in with their hearty Amens.

And then like the messengers of sudden death came the people of Umu-Ekogu. They rounded the kink in the road leading into the mission, brandishing machetes, clubs, and hoes. And without courtesy or ceremony or even a word of explanation, they hurled the coffin from the mouth of the ready grave and began hoeing loose earth back into the cavern.

Had the dead not earned their rest?

Did not the helpless deserve at least one act of deference?

There was a wild uproar. General discordance rising towards heaven. Scores of angry voices, speaking all at once. Physical contacts. Jostles. Pushes. Shoves.

Father Higler, agitated but in control of his priestly temper – often a surrogate of God's temper – is plucking the invaders by the shoulder and the elbow and asking: 'What do you want? What do you want? *Gini ka unu nacho?* What is the meaning of all this?'

Nwala, Philip's uncle, and the oldest man in the raiding party, snatches the candle out of the priest's hand and flings it high above the heads of the crowd into the bush. And the bush apprehended the light.

'You do not wish to be buried in there, White Man, do you?' Nwala asked.

The heathen does not get an answer. Father Higler breathes hard and fast. He and Nwala exchange stares of contempt not devoid of animosity. A fight has already broken out elsewhere in the crowd. Nwala whirls around and goes to it. The shoves and jostles of a few moments ago have graduated to blows. Scores of fights seem to have been spawned spontaneously. The older women and littler children, the weak, feckless and the uncommitted filter towards the relative safety of the periphery of the embattled crowd, ducking and side-stepping. There are no peace makers, only spectators and swingers.

The priest finds himself alone, the dead centre of the crowd's reckless swirl. He goes about shouting frenziedly, his face red, his beard bristling, his left hand still clutching his prayer book. 'Hey! Hey! Stop! Stop one moment! *Chere nu! Chere nu!*' But he could engage no one's attention. The devils in them understood neither English nor Igbo.

At length he found Philip and persisted until he got the servant's attention. 'What is the meaning of all this?' he demanded, as if Philip was responsible for everything, but Philip shrugged off the responsibility for an answer.

'What do they want?' Father Higler persisted. 'Where is your uncle? Has everybody gone mad?'

'Fada, me I do not know. I think they say they do not want us to bury Paul here.'

'Why not? What business is it of theirs?'

'The land beginning from here belongs to our compound. It is not common land like the rest of the mission. There is a boundary.'

'But all of it is idle forest. What could they possibly want with it? It is of no use to anyone. Can't you stop them? They are your people!'

They found Nwala.

'Fada want to know the reason for all this,' Philip said.

The breathless Nwala glared, then sent a shower of spit across Philip's face. 'Contempt stay with you!'

Suddenly galvanized, Philip seized Nwala by the throat. But his fingers froze. He munched his lips. His hands, then his whole body, began shaking.

'Hit me!' Nwala taunted. 'You are on their side, are you not? Go ahead and hit me, you the son of my own brother. Hit me!'

Philip let go of Nwala's neck and began to wipe the spit from his own face.

'Look at you,' Nwala pouted. 'Look at you! You have allowed them to dress you up in those fool's clothes. You who would not serve his own father's *Ihi Njoku*, now a pot boiler in the White Man's kitchen. Njoku Ekogu, consecrated to the biggest god that this land knows. You are asking me what we want? Standing there beside the wormy White Man? You do not know? I will tell you then, so you can tell your master . . .'

Before he could tell, two combatants came reeling into their midst. There was no time to jump sideways, so Father Higler backed away, stepping on what was left of the ridge that once surrounded the grave. The two were now on him. The only way he could avoid being knocked into the grave was to leap across it backwards. He did, getting the merest foothold on the other side. But as he tried to rise from his half-squat, the foothold gave and he fell into what was left of the grave. An avalanche of loose earth confirmed his fall, and for just one fleeting moment, a moment during which his stomach fluttered and his scalp tingled, he was seized by the morbid fear of being buried alive as Nwala had threatened. But the ever dutiful Philip reached down towards his outstretched hands and pulled him out.

What did they really want? he continued to ask. Why had they not come in peace, whatever was their reason for coming in the first place?

19

He got no answers, and the fights continued towards their appointed end. Spectators had gathered. Reinforcements had arrived on both sides. Some of the faithful, attempting a ruse, had assayed to dump the coffin unceremoniously into what was left of the original grave, knowing it would be exceedingly difficult to get it out again once it was in. But they had been caught in the effort and thwarted by the faithless. A tug of war had ensued, the coffin being heaved this way and that. At a point one end gave. One of the faithless fell backwards with the end piece clutched in both hands. A dubious trophy.

For a moment or two that unexpected eventuality cast a pall on everyone. The corpse's legs had slid out; the yellowed toes showed through the wrappings of burial cloth. The man who held the coffin's end-piece discarded his prize like a fearful thing, but as Paul's wife and son shrieked their dismay and rushed at him in concert, he picked it up again and used the jagged nails to hold them at bay.

The end of the fight was defeat for Father Higler and his congregation. The grave was closed, the coffin so battered that any further struggle would have caused its total collapse. There was little else to do now except to hurl threat and abuse and prolong the process of departure. And thus was completed the natural symmetry of this episode. Words at first had begotten blows. Now blows begot words again. Matthew, John and Genesis finished stuffing the legs of the corpse back into the coffin and with some others to help them, removed it to the base of an oil bean tree near the old church. On their part, Philip's jubilant relatives were savouring their victory, scraping around for loose earth which had become trampled all over – they still had about a foot of grave to fill.

But so does fate conspire to bury a worm in the juicy apple, and to cast her sands into the *garri* of the haughty. The victors had rushed into folly.

'*Ihe!*' Nwala exclaimed.

'*Ihem!*'

'*Ihem kwa!*' He twisted his shoulders in ritual pain.

'*Aru emela!*'

Silence descended upon them and their activities. One does not close a grave empty. It is not done! Hush! Immobility! They all understood. Even the faithful understood. One does not close a grave empty. It is neither healthful nor conducive to longevity. An empty grave is a hungry grave.

'Dig,' Nwala commanded. 'Dig it to its very first bottom. Bring my

20

Ofo bag. Get the trunk of a banana tree. Catch one of the rams and bring it here with my sharp machete.'

Shortly afterwards two young men returned with a banana trunk bridging their shoulders. Another followed with a ram on a leash and a two-faced machete in an embroidered goatskin sheath. A short time later, with all hands helping, the grave was opened again to its original depth.

Nwala began a ritual. All his kinsmen present – men, women and children – lined themselves around the grave in order of their ages. He circled the black *Ofo* stick around his own head and struck a powerful blow on the succulent banana trunk.

'Far be the tabu from my head!'

He straightened and cast his sight in the direction where the forlorn parishioners of St Peter Claver's were looking on hopelessly – their ranks whittled to Paul's closest relatives and a few of the most faithful, like Matthew, John and Genesis. Philip. Philip was next in age to Nwala, but he had defected from his upbringing, defaulted on his duties as Njoku – acolyte of the farm god. Nwala strode towards the group under the oil bean tree, and stopped before Philip – a tall and stout man with a sunken face, broad nose and deep eyes tucked under his heavy brows.

'My heart aches for you,' Nwala declared, exhaling and shaking his head at the misused servant in mass-server's vestments. 'Look! . . . Look at you! Look at what you have permitted them to do to you. You wear these things they put on little boys that have not yet shed their first teeth. For all the stature wasted on you! Tall like an iroko tree, marked from birth as if to become a chief. In the days when we were fighting for the land we now own you could have been expected to send a spear through two men at one throw, to cut off a man's head with one stroke of the machete. Amadioha! Why were you not still born? All your age mates have married three and four wives and fathered households of children. They are in the Yam Society and Okonko. But you, you prefer to be a pot boiler and sweep the White Man's kitchen with your testicles . . . Still you are one of us whether we like it or not. The blood that flows through us flows through you, even though yours has turned into sap. So I must do my duty.'

He raised the Ofo stick. Philip ducked and raised his hands above his head in a defensive move. But Nwala wanted only to circle the ritual stick around the servant's head. He did so, wheeled around and began striding away.

Back by the grave, Nwala completed the ceremony on the rest of his relatives. When the youngest child had been absolved they all joined hands to push the banana trunk into the grave.

'Grave, grave!' they shouted. 'Stay far from our compound! If you must have somebody, look somewhere else!'

The ram was then dragged to the graveside. Nwala drew his machete out of its sheath, tapped himself lightly on the hand with it, applied his mouth to the cut and drank the blood that came rushing forth. Then looking to the sky for the sun, he waved the machete at it and aimed a blow on the ram's neck.

Hark!

Geysers of blood. The severed head opens and closes its jaws in narrowing gaps, until finally they clasp firmly together – teeth bared between a snarl and a tormented laugh. The carcass thumps about a few times, and the feet kick headlessly, heedlessly, pointlessly, and then resolve to be still. The grave is drenched with blood.

Nwala drives his machete into the ground all the way to its hilt. He seizes the ram's head in both hands, raises it above his own head and forcefully hurls it into the grave.

'Close it!' he commands.

'They should not close it,' John was saying among the faithful. 'It is our grave. Genesis and me spent all morning digging it. They have no right to close it. I am not going to let it happen.' He walked forward, turned around a few steps later without breaking stride and said, 'Anyone who feels as I feel can come with me.'

Genesis followed him. Matthew followed. Then one of the ushers, Paul's widow and other relatives. Father Higler.

A new fight broke out. The people of Umu-Ekogu were hoeing earth into the last two and half feet of grave when John jumped into it and started scooping and flinging earth out of it with his hands, throwing it with great abandon into the faces of all those around him, both friend and foe.

A new crowd gathered. Men and women on their way to the farm or to the well stopped to watch and shake their heads. This phase of the fight, however, was destined for a short duration. One of Nwala's sons appeared suddenly from nowhere with a dane gun.

Everyone froze to a standstill. Nwala advanced towards the son, apparently no less surprised by the latest development than anyone else. The young man shrugged away from the father and moved to a different vantage point. 'Out of there!' he shouted. 'Or else they will bury you in there!' He aimed the gun at the grave, ostensibly at John. 'Out!'

There was a click as he pulled the hammer backwards to its full firing position.

'Do not shoot!' Nwala shouted. 'Do not shoot! Do you hear me? Get that gun from him! I say! . . .'

'Philip!' Father Higler shouted.

It was Philip who obeyed the order. He grabbed the weapon wielder from behind, and the two of them grappled for possession. They swung on it in see-saw motion, causing the crowd to run away from wherever the barrel pointed. Women shrieked. Children fell and were trampled.

There was a loud bang.

3

Father Higler was on his hands and on one knee. He had tried to leap sideways when he saw the barrel of the gun pointing in his direction, but he caught the tail of his soutane under his heel and had fallen. That fall had saved his life, for the gun barrel had suddenly swooped upwards in an oblique path as Philip made an energetic swing to wrest it from his cousin. The gun had discharged at that very moment.

Nwala, a few moments behind the priest, had tried to duck but had not been quick enough. A glancing barrage of shot – broken nails and assorted scraps of metal – had hit his left abdomen and his left hand, stopped him in his tracks. He was wounded but not dead.

It was John, the erstwhile grave digger, who did not survive a barrage of shots on his face and chest. He had been on his way to assist Father Higler in case Nwala attacked the priest.

Father Higler was momentarily numbed by the discharge which had taken place hardly ten feet from him. His consciousness was temporarily suspended and the faculties of his mind seemed to lose their cohesion. He was regressed to that awful day in the fields of Verdun when his courage had sagged and then buckled. Now as then, the outer world had been darkened, he could neither hear nor see. But there were no inner lights now, no flashes of insight and no inner voices as there had been on that other woeful battlefield. It was dark here all over, inside and outside him. His mind was horribly darkened – devoid of all thought and imagination, truant to its functions.

But then he slowly became aware of time's passage. He was alive. At length he could smell the acridity of the gunpowder. And then suddenly the voices of the surrounding confusion burst on him – shrieks, wailings, moans, curses. He recovered enough will to urge his eyes open, and he could see the grass under him, his own muddied hands and vestments, the prayer book which somehow he still clutched. For a moment he wished it were true, as some of his parishioners believed, that to own a prayer book was to be in command of all the prayers therein, so he could send them all to heaven in one breath.

He saw Philip approaching. The servant offered a hand and helped him up.

Fate, he thought, stalked her victims with the guile and patience of the seasoned hunter, nudging them toward the abyss until they took the lethal step. Fate then sat back, pinched herself and laughed uproariously – at the child who would not stop until it had caressed the glittering edge of the razor or who would take no dissuasion until it had tested its fingers on the beautiful, glowing piece of hot iron. The cut, the burn, the agonized cry. Who was to blame? To whom did the aliases belong?

With the gun blast, a sudden chill had taken possession of every flaring temper among the fighters. Everyone seemed suddenly tired. It appeared that the gun blast was what they all had been working for and waiting for, not just since they started fighting that afternoon, but all that morning, even the previous day, week, year – all their lives. It was as if their flaring tempers had achieved a momentary orgasm, as if suddenly they had been doused with icy water from the sky, as if an unchallengeable referee had blown a final whistle – stop action! – on them, and they had no choice but to obey.

Nwala was carried off by his relatives – for the well-begotten, incapacity is a private thing. John lay dying in the grass.

'Put something under his head to raise it up.'

'Make an act of contrition in his ear, Philip.'

'*Miseratur tui omnipotens Deus et dimissis peccatis tuis, perducat te ad vitam aeternam!*'

'Amen!'

'That is it,' Matthew said. 'He is gone.'

'Somebody give me a hand,' Genesis said, shoving himself past the others to get to the corpse. 'He must not lie here in public view.'

Father Higler tried to remember when last he had heard John's confession but could not. He squeezed his prayer book hard. He had a feeling that tears were coming to the ends of his eyes. 'God! God!' He entered the little chapel but discovered that he could not pray coherently. He strained to rouse his conscience, to focus his attention on the tabernacle and concentrate so hard on it that everything else would be blurred out of existence. But his eyes seemed to have an irresistible propensity to stray, and when they did not stray, they became fatigued from the forced and unblinking gaze. Worse still, his ears reached outside and pulled in sounds he did not wish to hear, and his mind eagerly registered them, sorted them and classified them into their appropriate places in relation to the events of that terrible day. There was the twitter of birds, and the sounds of children at play, children insensitive of the cares of adulthood, and there were the distant sounds of the conversations of people who had stopped to inspect the site of the fighting.

Suddenly he heard Philip's voice telling someone that he could not be seen that day. He repressed the urge to go out.

'He is not at home?' the voice asked.

'He is at home,' Philip said.

'In sleep?'

'What it matters to you whether he is in sleep or not? He cannot see you today. Finish.'

The stranger left, and shortly afterwards there were the sounds of Philip washing plates. Then he was breaking wood. That eternal servant! Who could it be that had just been talking to him? Someone desiring to be baptized? To go to confession? Someone with a premonition of his own death? Someone about to die of a freak accident like the one that had claimed John that afternoon? Without confession? 'Oh God of God! Supreme Majesty! Infinite Wisdom! Justice! Mercy!' He repeated the name over and over under his breath. The divine adjectives tumbled out of his mouth like unsettled pebbles down a mountain pass. But they were just words, desperate words, lacking the faith to buoy them to heaven.

'Who is that? Go away. Fada see no person again today!' That was Philip's voice once more.

'Filipu!'

'Oh, it is you, Mista Matthew.' Matthew was Paul's supposed successor.

'Yes.'

'I am sorry. Fada says no one again today can see him.'

'Tell him it is *me*,' Matthew said importantly.

'The way he said it,' Philip replied, 'it is like even if his mother rises from the dead now-now and wants to see him, he cannot see her too.'

Yes, indeed, Father Higler thought. Philip was making a condition of a most improbable miracle. For his mother was lying quietly in her grave beside his father in the churchyard of Saint John in that little village fourteen miles from Obernai which was once his home. Four or five thousand miles away. It was cold up there now. Perhaps there was a little snow on the ground, thinly smearing the grass in the cemetery and frosting the headstones. And with All Soul's Day just a few days past, there would be recently wilted flowers on many of the graves and little mounds of freshly burned candle wax, perhaps one distraught woman visiting the new grave of a husband recently deceased.

There would be no flowers on his parents' graves, and there would have been no one to visit them for ten, fifteen years? They were perhaps two of the most forlorn buried there. But then they had each other for company. He had no one here.

Not far away was old Saint John's church, dilapidated but defiant, with its narrow tinted windows, its foot-worn steps and heavy oak doors with tarnished brass handles. On weekday afternoons like today, it was a desolate place with no signs of life or current use unless one of the old women through with her novenas crawled out of it. But those women gave little sign of life. Hunched, tottering, heavily covered even on warm days, they seemed more like honoured dead parishioners crawling out of their places of internment in the crypt.

'God! God! God!'

He struggled with all his strength to conjure God down, to fetch Him from heaven into that mud-walled, thatch-roofed chapel. God, however, remained elsewhere far away – as far away it seemed as Europe, where He was held prisoner in the cathedrals. God seemed to belong more appropriately in Europe, to fit more nicely and naturally – a stately, old white man resembling the legendary Saint Nicholas, with a flowing white beard and an eye cocked like a Swiss watchmaker on the tangling fabric of the universe he had fashioned. Those cathedrals, many of them with rosters of canonized saints securely in heaven, seemed natural enough places to find God. On the other hand, God seemed to have created Africa and fled from its heat and its jungles and from the savages He had placed thereon, and if He were to show up unannounced in that little chapel or on Sunday among the sweaty, black faces that knelt in church, He would look very strange indeed.

When at long last Father Higler released himself from the chapel, Philip rushed forward to minister to him.

'Boil me some bath water.'

'Already I have boiled.'

'How is your uncle?'

'He is not dead, Fada.'

'H'm. Is he in a bad way?'

'The wound is on the side of his belly. It may or may not kill him. That is up to God now.'

'Which God?' Father Higler felt prompted to ask. Which God was jealous of Nwala's health? But he banished the thought with a rebuke to himself. 'Will they make more trouble, do you think?'

'I no think so, Fada. Everybody now bellyful with trouble.'

Philip picked a bucket of hot water off the fire and walked with it into the bath shelter where he emptied it into a tin tub. Then he fetched a bucket of cold water which he added in measured amounts to the tub.

Father Higler stepped into the tub, lowered himself gingerly, lay back as far as he could. When the water became tepid, he began to soap himself.

He could hear Philip talking to some children. 'I am not cooking today,' he was telling them. 'So all of you can go away and not make noise to disturb Fada. Didn't you see what happened today?'

'You kill a fowl tomorrow?'

'If you mother gives it to me, I will! I said go. Go now!'

The silence suggested the children were on their way, but then they must have stopped for after a while he heard their voices again.

'Remember the wood I bring for you that time three yesterdays ago? You said for that the stomach things of your next fowl belong to me.'

'Go now! . . . Come to catechism tomorrow. Maybe I kill fowl then.'

'You will?'

'Yes. If you go now and come to mass and catechism tomorrow.'

'But me, was it not me you promised the stomach things the other time when I brought water for you from the well. And the feet too you said you would give to me.'

'I have said go! If you do not go now-now none of you will get anything when I kill the fowl. I will call a dog and with you watching feed everything to him.'

Silence.

Had it not been written that the bread of the children must not be thrown to the dogs?

Was it not in the Book that the children of this world are wiser than the children of the kingdom?

And so it was then that Philip deferred the promises and postponed the debts, half-paying from time to time to keep the hopes alive, dangling the arrears before the hungry eyes. The head and the stomach things, the disposable whatnots, the clawed, scaly feet, lent their weight and their juices to the advancement of God's work as Philip used them to lure the children to morning mass, catechism classes, and choir practice. On the rare occasion when someone gifted Father Higler with a goat or sheep, there were bones to be cracked for marrow and yards and yards of intestines, quarts of blood, pounds of whatnots. The cleaning, the mincing and chopping, the seasoning with pepper and spices. And then the coils of intestine – *mirabile visu* – turned into coils of delectable sausage. Cooked and dried, every inch was worth a bundle of firewood, a bucket of water or a child's presence at mass or catechism.

'Why don't you sleep here tonight?' Father Higler counselled. 'You could make yourself a cot in the corner over there.'

'Fada, what about tomorrow? And next tomorrow? Will I live here the rest of my life?'

'Worry about the rest of your life only when you're sure you have it coming.'

'Fada, I am not a child anymore. At a point a man has to stop running and say to what is after him: Here I am! What about it?'

'Discretion, Philip. Discretion. The devil is alive in those relatives of yours. I saw him only too clearly this afternoon.'

'In me too. I have a devil inside me.'

'Akhee-khee-khee . . .' Old Ahamba says. 'Insanity tugs at all of us. Akhee-khee-khee . . .'

Father Higler said nothing more, went into his bedroom to don his soutane and came out shortly raking a comb across his sparse hair. Gaunt shadows which the late afternoon sun sketched from the rubber and oil bean trees lay across the mission. The atmosphere was quiet and there was a thin blue-tinted haze in the air, the sort of haze characteristic of the harmattan. Two women with empty straw baskets on their heads and a girl of sixteen or seventeen were gazing at the scene of the fight. As he watched, he recognized the girl as Philip's daughter. A half-wit, physically over-endowed, she was actually a cousin or niece of some sort whose mother had been assigned to Philip at the death of some relative. But Philip had laid no claim to this bequest even if the girl called him 'nna'.

'See? See?' the girl was saying, touching her toes to the edge of the grave. 'See? I did it.'

She apparently had been wagered something by the women to dare to go near the grave.

'See? See? Nothing has happened to me.'

'What Fada want me to cook for supper?'

'I don't want any supper, Philip.'

'Fada, you never eat anything since morning time.'

'I know. Look, Philip, I think you better stay here tonight.'

Philip's face and lips made several starts, but eventually his disagreement was not spoken. Later that evening he quietly left. Father Higler sat on the edge of his *agada*, a bed of raffia fronds, a mattress of jute sacks stuffed with cotton from the giant cottonwood trees which shed their cotton in March. He removed his shoes, soutane and shorts and lay down. Bed so early? he half asked himself. He did not answer and avoided all thought and conscious decision.

All that night he slept fitfully, tossing and rolling between snatches of somnolence in which fragmented memories from his past and from the passing day mingled with the exaggerated reality of the night noises outside his window to produce hideous nightmares. Prancing monstrosities seemed to lurk everywhere in the room. A clangour that seemed to belong to another world filled his ears. John's face assaulted him, that face in its death throes, black and drawn and beaded with oily sweat and jarred as if with great apprehension. Two front teeth were missing from the upper jaw of the gaping mouth, but it was the eyes that he recalled most vividly as they were dilated, caught in a wild stare between puzzlement and exclamation, seeking a permanent focus, but meanwhile focused on nothing. His powerlessness to be of help to John at that moment, physically or spiritually! Did Satan get him?

He picked up his rosary from the bedpost and squeezed it, wished he had a gun. Then perhaps he could feel himself as a source of power – some power was better than no power at all – against the amorphous, the generalized and the impalpably palpable dangers that threatened him. He had no power over the inner tumult, nor the outer tumult, no command and no command post. He could not even enjoin his own mind to observe the peace and be still. A gun. What mockery! Had he not flung away the last gun he had held and fled in hysteria pursued by cowardice. What would he do with a gun now – shoot it point-blank into the darkness without? And within? Was he not a priest? Was his strength not supposed to come from the spirit? Was the Lord himself not present in the Blessed Sacrament in his chapel just a few yards away?

Tu es sarcedos in aeternum!

Ah yes, a priest forever. Chosen but not marked. Sent but not armed. Marooned without reprieve. These signs shall follow them that believe in me. Nothing. Nothing. Nothing.

The sun was already up when he awakened the next morning. Philip heard him and put some water on the washstand. His face was tender. He immersed it in the cold water and felt better. He had a sprain in every joint. He towelled and dressed. Then he picked up a notebook with ruled pages, his diary, and wrote down the date. Then he paused to collect his thoughts, stared at the paper for a long time and finally skidded to a start, writing effusively, explaining and exonerating himself.

Finally he stepped out on the veranda, and Africa – he always thought of the village as Africa – was well awake and gloriously alert in the morning sun. It was the same every morning. People, goats, sheep, insects and birds, the sun, the rain, or the convulsing clouds, they were there already in the middle of their habitual preoccupations. Waking up to them every morning was like seeing actors on a stage which had been made ready under cover of darkness and then suddenly lit. It was as if nobody and nothing had gone to sleep since the previous day.

4

There were about a dozen people at mass that morning, a combined requiem for the faithful dead. Father Higler performed the ceremony with seasoned efficiency, manipulating his prayers and rituals with dexterity, with Philip as his server. The faithful batted their eyes and grunted their amens.

Breakfast. Two peeled oranges. Toast, or roasted bread, as Philip called it. One egg. Tea.

'Fada want more tea?'

'No, Philip. But you can bring me more roasted bread.'

Philip returned in a little while with three slices of toast.

'So you went home after all last night.'

'Yes, Fada.'

'How is your uncle?'

'Still alive, Fada.'

'Is he any better or worse?'

'In between both.'

'Do you at all pray for them, Philip? I mean all your relatives?'

'Myself I need a lot of prayers.'

'We all need prayers, Philip. Still we pray for one another. It is said that no one goes to heaven alone, just as no one goes to hell alone. You have been given the gift of faith. You are the light of that compound. You cannot put your light under the bed or in a bushel ... Ah yes, that reminds me. What about your daughter?'

'My daughter?'

'Yes. Ugochi. It just occurred to me she does not attend catechism. She should be baptized, don't you think?'

'Yes Fada.'

'Why don't you bring her then to catechism?'

'Fada, I do not know if she can learn.'

'We can find out. You might be surprised.'

'But Fada I fear she will make the other children to laugh in catechism class. They always laugh at her because of the way she is.'

'Well, maybe you can teach her in private. You are her foster-father and our catechist. In either capacity you owe her a duty.'

'Fada, people like her need baptism too? God will judge them too?'

'She too has a soul, Philip. A soul like mine and yours, which must be saved.'

'God can send somebody like her with only half a mind to hell?'

'We don't know what God will do, Philip. We do what we can in faith. And we go on hoping.'

The dead were committed to rest amidst songs, wailing and gun blasts, Paul first, then John, each on his own compound. The burials took up most of the day.

Father Higler spent the evening in his garden, boxed in by a hedge on the southwest corner of the rectory just outside the fence of palm fronds which kept the sheep and goats out of the backyard and Philip's kitchen.

'Philip!'

'Yes Fada.'

'Bring me a bucket of water that I can use for watering the flowers.'

'Yes Fada.'

Philip carried a bucket of clean water to the break in the hedge which was the entrance to the garden. 'Fada, I cannot find the cup.'

'I used it only last week. Did you look in the woodshed?'

'Yes Fada. And it was not there.'

'Get me another cup then.'

'Yes Fada.'

'Use a small nail for punching the holes.'

'All right, Fada.'

Philip went away, and shortly afterwards Father Higler could hear him as with a nail he punched holes in the bottom of an old cigarette tin. This tin he would use as a sprinkler for watering the flowers.

The balsams and zinnias needed mainly water. They had only very little growth left in them and put out only a few sickly flowers. The soil around them was dry and crusty. Really fertile soil was hard to come by here and even harder to keep. The rains in August and September leached the manure he poured around them. The sun in late October and early November pulverized what was left. Only the hardiest plants survived the harmattan in December.

He was a good gardener. In fact, he had begun his priestly career as a gardener. When he found himself in England after his desertion, he had had to prove that he really had a vocation to the priesthood by working for a year as a gardener in Saint Mary's Seminary.

He thought of those years at Saint Mary's, especially that first day when he had met Father Morris, the impression he had had of himself as a fraud, his attempt to look respectable, and the belying drab and out-of-season suit which he had bought for himself in a second-hand store. He had confessed himself to Father Morris, and afterwards requested an interview where he related his intentions.

'You will understand, of course,' Father Morris declared, 'that a man cannot walk in here, no history behind him, and ask to become admitted to the seminary. How do we know? . . .' He had paused and looked at him, then repeated the question. 'How do we know that . . .?'

'That I am not a fraud?'

'Well, yes. At least in a way, though I would not use that particular word.' He paused, then added, 'Of course you don't present yourself one day and become ordained the next. You would have many years in which to prove yourself. Did you realize that?'

'Yes, Father.'

'Obviously you are not English.'

'No.'

'German?'

'No, French. Alsatian.'

'I see.'

They began speaking in French, and he felt great relief at not having to stutter in English.

'What is your name?'

'Anton Higler.'

'I am Father John Morris. You are not a spy or anything? There is a war going on.'

'No, I am not a spy.'

'A fugitive from justice? You have not committed a crime?'

'No. I have committed no crime.'

'How long have you been in England?'

'About ten days.'

Father Morris looked up at him suddenly, then dismissed his surprise and cast his head down thoughtfully. They walked along a gravelled path, surrounded by the peace and serenity of a cloistered environment. The path took a dive towards a lake, a placid pool circumscribed by ancient elms. 'That over there,' Father Morris pointed out to him, 'was the first building on this site. It is three hundred and seventy-five years old this year . . .'

'I see.'

For a few moments they stood beside the lake in silence. On the southeast edge two mother ducks were leading their families in paddling processions. Then a group of black-habited seminarians had been disgorged from a building to their right and had begun scattering themselves over the premises in twos and threes. A few solitary ones with their eyes glued to prayer books began pacing the path that ran along the edge of the lake.

Father Morris then spoke once more. 'You were not in the war?' His voice bore a hint of suspicion.

'Yes, I was in the war.'

'Oh! What happened?'

The explanation gummed itself to his throat.

Father Morris looked up at him and his cold, discerning gaze suppressed the courage which for a moment had seemed about to welter up in his heart.

'Father,' he said then. 'To put it simply. I am not there anymore.'

'That seems obvious enough,' Father Morris said. 'But what exactly happened? Why did you leave the army? How did you get here?'

'I left the army, Father.'

'Yes, you must have,' Father Morris said, showing a gift of infinite patience. 'But why?'

'To become a priest.'

Father Morris suspended his interrogation temporarily, and the two of them watched two seminarians, both in khaki trousers rolled up to their knees make ready to launch a boat from a little pier some three hundred yards away. A third seminarian called to them, gathered his soutane around his waist and climbed on board. The boat heaved dangerously, threatening to throw off its latest passenger, but he was a good sailor and balanced himself adroitly, then took his time sitting down. Father Morris, who had opened his mouth and raised his hand in silent alarm, heaved a breath of relief and shook his head.

'You were born a Catholic?'

'Yes.'

'Are your parents in Alsace?'

'They are both dead.'

'Catholic?'

'Yes.'

'You know what a vocation is?'

'Yes.'

'And you think you have one?'

'Yes.'

'Since when have you thought so?'

He figured the days in his mind, and then replied. 'Three weeks.'

'What happened to you three weeks ago? How did you reach your decision? You are a mature man, of course, and well above the age at which we admit most of our novices. So one would be inclined to give your decision more weight than usual. Nevertheless, if all of a sudden, three weeks ago, you thought you should become a priest, one feels impelled to ask you to explain further. Tell me, had you ever thought you might have a vocation before three weeks ago?'

'Yes, Father. When I was much younger. The usual fancies, I imagine, that every young Catholic boy has as an altar boy.'

'But never in your adult life? Nothing more than a boyhood fancy before three weeks ago?'

'No.'

'How does one know that three weeks from now you won't suddenly decide *not* to become a priest?'

'I am quite sure I will not make such a decision.'

'And before three weeks ago, you were sure you did not want to become a priest, weren't you?'

'I don't think it is the same thing, Father.'

'What type of work did you do before joining the army?'

'I was a grocer.'

'Go to school much?'

'Some. I was in the lycée for three years.'

'Well,' Father Morris said, and seemed either resolved or to have run out of questions. He folded his hands behind his back and began a childish, rolling, side-to-side swagger. 'You have papers, I presume?'

'Yes, I have some papers.'

'And you don't have a living wife here or in Alsace?'

'No.'

'Regarding your papers, it is not that we care particularly about such things, but there are laws of course about these things, and besides there is a war going on. What rank were you in the army, Major? Colonel?' There was an uncharitable tease in his voice.

'Corporal,' he said. 'I volunteered.'

'Exactly when did you leave the army?'

'Three weeks ago.'

Father Morris was startled. 'You mean the same time you had your vocation?' he asked.

'Yes.'

'You mean? – You mean, you mean you are a deserter?'

'Yes!' After that admission he had a feeling of sinking lower and lower towards the earth, and a craving for the earth to open up and swallow him. That had been the very first time he had admitted to anyone, including himself, that he had deserted from the army under fire. Before this he had thought himself as striking a perfectly honourable deal with God. But after Father Morris had used that word, he had felt cowardice written all over him.

Bravery! Bravery and death were partners in the war. One had to die to prove that one was brave. Why should he have been expected to choose death simply because the rulers of Europe had decided that their honours were at stake and were prepared to slaughter hundreds of thousands of people to prove themselves serious? But nobody seemed to understand, not even the Spiritual Director of a seminary.

He scraped the last of the water out of the bucket and got up from his squat and called: 'Philip!'

'Fada!'

'Make my bath water ready.'

'Already ready Fada.'

Fatigue. The feeling of dissipation, emptying out, waste, void. The greatest liability of human nature is an imagination that far outstrips other capacities. Nature's cruel trick, further compounded by the capacity to reflect, to stand aside and be a spectator of self and friends, a witness to the yawning hiatus between possibility and actuality.

He bathed, supped, stopped in the chapel briefly and then went for a walk around the premises. The new church – new because it was still not far from where it had started. Only the topmost layer of bricks was new, the rest were already relics. A relic builder, he! He put his breviary aside and arranged a row of recently moulded bricks into a pile.

'Good even, Fada.'

'Good evening.' He straightened and peered. 'Ah, Matthew.' Matthew was head of the church committee now that Paul was dead.

'Yes Fada. How is Fada?'

'Fada is fine. How are you?'

Matthew shrugged his shoulders indifferently, switched his lips to one side, lips red like a trumpeter's and overhung by a moustache.

Father Higler clapped his hands free of dust. Well? . . .'

'Fada I have something I wish to talk about.'

'What is it, Matthew? Let's hear it.'

'It is about yesterday.'

A deep grunt. 'H'm.'

'It is my thought that we should do something about the people of Umu-Ekogu. What they did yesterday to make a fight on us when we were mourning a corpse should not pass without challenge.'

'H'm, I don't know, Matthew. I don't think so. What can we do? Give them a return fight? We have had enough fighting, don't you think? What useful purpose could it possibly serve to start over now? One man is already dead as a result of yesterday.'

'Our own man, Fada. It was our own man who died. And John was a good man. A good Christian man.'

'Agreed. But he is dead.'

'We can just bury him and forget him? How and why he died? How can his spirit rest in peace seeing how it seems he died in vain?'

'No one who dies in the faith dies in vain. Did Our Lord himself die in vain because he allowed his enemies to crucify him? No, Matthew, what we can now do for John is remember him in our prayers and masses, and ask almighty God to shorten his days in purgatory. As for ourselves we need the strength to fight the fight that matters, to do good and avoid sin, to bear our crosses and to merit the grace of final repentance, and when our time comes, a happy death.'

'And the people of Umu-Ekogu?'

'God will deal with them according to his infinite mercy. And his justice. We can only pray for them.'

'We pray for them? What difference then between us and them? On which side is God and justice? Where is our advantage?'

'Not in this world, Matthew. It is a hard lesson to learn, but *that* is the lesson. Our way here is the way of peace, regardless of what others do. We must, each of us and all of us together, become instruments of God's peace. Like Saint Francis. Have you heard the story of Saint Francis?'

'No.'

'I must tell you about him some day. He was a staunch exemplar of the spirit of peace. We all need peace, Matthew. Within us and around us.'

'But how can we get peace unless those around us also want peace?'

'Hard. But we can. They can learn from our example.'

'Fada, maybe the church committee can meet after mass on Sunday.'

'Why? What for?'

'To talk.'

'Make our plans for peace? Or is it war, Matthew, that you have in mind?' He sighed. 'The masons did not show again today. I need someone with a bicycle to go and seek them out tomorrow.'

'Perhaps Genesis.'

'Yes, Genesis perhaps. We must hurry this church. You think we'll ever complete it?'

'In time, Fada. It is up to God.'

'It is all up to God, yes. Everything. Everything is up to God. He is our refuge, our last resort . . . Even our peace. *Udo*, is that not the word?'

'*Ndokwa.*'

'Yes. *Ndokwa diri unu*, is that what you say? Or is it *Udo diri unu*? What is the difference?'

'*Udo* is peace on the outside. No fight or war. Happy calmness in the village and town. *Ndokwa* is well-being. Satisfaction of the heart. Peace of the mind, inside. *Udo* is for the community. *Ndokwa* is for the person.'

'I see. We need both *udo* and *ndokwa*. And we can make our church a symbol of the new peace of mind and body, and community, rising above all tumult, whether internal or external.'

'Has Fada heard that the Village Council will hold a judgement about yesterday?'

'They will?'

'Yes Fada. That is one reason we must meet.'

'Do we have anything to fear?'

'Not if we put our ears to the ground and remain solicitous.'

'Look to it, Matthew. I know we can rely on you.'

'What I do for our church I do for myself, Fada. That is the way I see it.'

'That's the spirit. I will see you tomorrow then.'

'Yes Fada.'

'Please see if you can contact Genesis.'

'Yes Fada. Goodnight Fada.'

'Goodnight Matthew.'

Each of them began walking off in his own direction in the dim light. Father Higler sighed. 'Peace, Oh God, peace!'

Woe is me that I sojourn in Mosoch
That I dwell among the tents of Cedar!
All too long I've dwelt with those who hate peace
When I speak peace, they're ready for war.

The next morning, a persistent knocking awakened him. It could not be Philip. Philip rarely had a reason to wake him up so early. No twitter yet of dawn birds. No rarefaction of the darkness. The room was solidly black and not in its dawn penumbra. He struck a match and lit the lamp, donned his shorts, walked out to his living room and then to the veranda.

'Hello. Who is there?' Peering.

'White Man . . .'

'Ah, my good friend. Is that you?'

'Hmmmh. And how is your health?'

'Fair. How about you?'

'Just as you see me.'

'I cannot see you.' Raising the lamp above his head, peering intently into the darkness beyond the circle of the lamp's light. 'Come into the light. Why are you staying out there?'

'I stay where I am. And I like the morning's dew on my rheumatism. Hold the lamp down.'

'Well, you woke me up ...'

'I did, White Man? You really are awake now? Ah, well, that is good. It is good to be awake in both eyes.'

'It's really too early in the morning for riddles. And I don't relish standing here. If I may ask, to what do I owe the honour of this unusual visit?'

'Your health. I came to inquire about your health.'

'I am surviving, thank you.'

'Good. Do not slumber too deeply, or with both eyes, unless you know who else is asleep. Especially your enemies.'

'I have no enemies that I know of.'

'Ah, but you see, our enemies are like the people who seduce our wives. They know us, not we them. Akhee-khee-khee!'

'Are you by any chance talking about the incident with Nwala and his friends?'

'That is a question. You like to ask questions.'

'I like to get answers. But you are full of riddles. I say it is too early in the morning, and my sleep has been breached. You must have a good reason for coming.'

'Khee-khee! We get no answers, all of us. Life is full of riddles. I did not make them. How can I solve them?'

'Are you on your way somewhere?'

'Or on my way from somewhere?'

'Whichever. But I wish I knew the meaning of this rigmarole. I infer you are trying to tell me something you think I should know. What is it?'

'There again a question. You ask questions like a child, White Man. Is that the way it is where you come from? Then tell me this: Why is the night dark and the day light? Why does the river flow down the mountain and not up ... Akhee-khee-khee ... All I say is: Look about you.'

'There is nothing to see. I see nothing that should matter. Nothing.'

'Then look again. Or get someone who sees to see for you.'

'A seer?'

'Someone who sees.'

'But if there is nothing to see?'

'Then keep looking. But I must go. It grows light.'

'Come and visit me some evening when you have fewer riddles, or are prepared to unravel them yourself. I hope you can do so soon.'

'Akhee-khee. Are we not all held together by our hopes?'

Genesis came to mass that morning. Announced to Father Higler that his wife was pregnant.

'Thanks to God!'

But what would she bear?

'Be hopeful, Genesis, but don't you put God to the test.'

'Why? Because he might fail?'

'No. Because you might fail. The test will rebound on your faith. Have faith. And hope.'

'I hope she delivers the correct kind of child.'

'All gifts are from God. Hope, yes, but better still trust in God's superior judgement.'

Genesis was dispatched in search of the masons.

Philip reported Nwala worse. Sleepless, and delirious.

'Is he going to die?'

'I don't know, Fada. But he is not getting better.'

Father Higler could not miss the emphasis in Philip's voice, a voice not commonly demonstrative. Nor did he fail to note the strain on the servant's face all through the day.

'Perhaps you can try to baptize him, Philip.'

'Fada they will not even allow me into the room where he is lying.'

'You have not really seen him then?'

'No Fada, but I have heard him.'

'Perhaps I'll go and see him myself.'

'Fada should be careful.'

'Why? What's there to fear?'

'I do not know, but I still think Fada should look about him.'

'What's the whole idea, anyway? Everyone, it seems, wants me to look about me. What is there about me? What is there to see?'

Philip shrugged.

Afternoon. The routines returned. He took a siesta. The sound of Philip's tom-tom for catechism classes awakened him about three-thirty. But he lolled in bed, listening to the noisy class proceed from simpler questions whose answers all the children knew to the more difficult and newer ones.

Philip: 'Is there God?'

Children: 'Yes, there is God.'

Philip: 'Does God have a beginning or end?'

Children: 'No, God has no beginning or end. He has always been, still is, and forever will continue to be.'

Philip: 'How many Gods are there?'

Child: 'Three! The Father, the Son and the Holy Ghost!'

Giggles. Philip's harsh voice correcting the misimpression. There was only one God – the Father, the Son and the Holy Ghost were all one and the same God.

'Repeat after me, There is only one God!'

Again!

Again!

Philip: 'Where does God live?'

Children: 'God lives in heaven.'

Philip: 'Where is God?'

Children: 'God is everywhere.'

After catechism came the choir practice. Christmas was not very far off. Father Higler arose and helped with some of the Latin songs.

Later that night when he was alone in bed, he thought about different people – Philip, Matthew, Genesis, Paul's widow and children. The new church. Himself. He was a terminal bud. Fifty-three years old. Seventeen years to his three-score-and-ten, if that quota was not abridged. He was ageing. He did not have much time. In a few years he would be dead. Quietly and obscurely dead. Had he lived in vain? He could not marry. He could not have a son who would bear his name and try through another lifetime to put a mark on the featureless passage of generations of Higlers. He was truly a terminal bud. Or did it matter at all?

There was hope in the new church. It would one day be complete, please God! He would prepare for himself a place of internment near its altar. *Hic Jacet* – the Reverend Anton Higler.

Vainglorious?

Wasn't this labourer worthy of the most meagre hire?

Our glass empties
Momentum begets entropy
Uncertain life careens to certain death

He fell asleep.

5

The Village Assembly appointed a day to probe the events at Paul's funeral and John's subsequent death. Matthew had been correct after all, and this eventuality had also been the true meaning of Old Man Ahamba's cryptic allusions. The day was *Orie*; the village's eight-day market would be in session that evening, but the judgement was in the morning, at the market concourse, under the large cottonwood trees, beside the fetish huts and juju shrines. The trees were girdled with young palm leaves; some bore the imprint of smashed eggs, and still others were smeared with the blood of sacrificed animals.

All that morning – in fact much of the day before, the village had hummed with palpable tension. There was more traffic on the footpaths, much of it more hurried than usual. Oblique and circumlocutious talk. Studied restraint. Earnest whispers. The imminence of something important. At about bedtime the *uhie*, wooden master gong, had sounded to remind everyone of the assembly the following morning. Its tone was urgent.

Midmorning. The sun had dried the night dew off the grass and sketched vague shadows only a little longer than life size. The early grass-hoppers were beginning to snap, the dried andropogons to crackle. Men arrived at the concourse and took their places around the big tree. Solemn old men with leathery skins and shaved heads, exotic tattoos and body indigoes, jangling bracelets and anklets, young men in *ukpo* and Madras cotton loin cloths dyed in earth colours. Some sat on the logs, some on the bare ground, some on padded tripods which they had brought along, others on goatskins and still others on leaves which they spread on the dust. There was general banter, irrelevant to the issue at hand, while bowls of kola nuts and pepper seeds were introduced, celebrated according to custom and passed around, and the palm wine flowed from earthenware jars and huge calabashes.

At length the sound of the *ogele* – king-kong, king-kong, king-kong ... The din subsides. The assembly is formally opened by Old Man

Ahamba at his circumlocutious best, casting far and wide for the most far-flung allusions and spinning riddles to explain other riddles. Almost immediately afterwards, an issue arose: Should the White Man be seated at the assembly and be allowed to speak?

No!

Certainly not!

No, he is not of this soil! Not one of us!

He is strange to us and we to him!

He will not speak? Does he not eat from his mouth and like us to go to pot from the other end?

Why should he speak, a mere stranger?

Who will speak for him if he does not speak for himself?

Yes, he has been gifted with his own lips, so let him speak!

And he has learned to use our tongue. Not like the D. O. (District Officer) who needs *ntaprinta* (interpreter)!

Since he has lived here, has he caused us any trouble?

He helped us to get the well, and now our wives and children do not have to trek far for water.

That is correct. He talked to the D. O. and the well came to us.

Let him speak because we are just.

He will speak because it is no show of strength to maltreat a hapless stranger.

He is our refugee, and we hold refugees sacred.

He lives on the fruits of our bushes and the produce of our land, so let him speak.

Because our justice must be like the brittle twig which admits no bending, he can speak.

Ahamba: He will speak then! *Amala, unu ekwela nu?*

(Community, have you all agreed?)

Zem!

Kwenu!

Zem!

While the agreement was still being ratified by low murmurs and silent gestures, Genesis rises, and surveying the crowd says: 'Before we go on, should we not say why we are here? Is that not proper? So that everyone knows?'

Ahamba, interrupting: 'Who is that? Who are you, boy? And where did you just come from?' A bitter chuckle. A pause to administer a depreciating scowl. 'Assembly, did you hear him? He wants to know why we are here. Clearly then he does not know. He is not connected, and it is said that those who do not know never know. Listen, young man, where did you get your dare, the courage to rise in the face of this assembly, seeing who else is here? Your dead father would not have dared to do it – and he was much better begotten than you have turned out to be.'

Genesis protests, 'I will have nothing said against my father. You knew him!'

'Yes, I knew him,' Ahamba retorts. 'There are men here now greater than him in life, greater than him in death. A man's death is as big as his life, no bigger.'

'No man . . .'

'Are you interrupting me?' Ahamba glares. His old eyes light like flares. His beard flickers up and down. 'Amadike, are you here?'

'Here!'

'Ogbudimkpa, are you here?'

'Here!'

'Aguneri, are you here?'

'Here!'

'Those are three sons of mine about your age. You are a child hardly out of your mother's womb. The snot is still running from your nose. You have but one wife, and have yet to father a son. And then you have the courage to look me in the face and ask the cheeky question . . . You three boys watch him! If you catch his lips moving, take him out and shove a good handful of sand down his throat.' A mirthless chuckle. '*Amala kwenu!*'

Zem!

Kwenu!

Zem!

'The White man has turned our nights into day and our days into night. But we are still here – here when he came, here too when he will again leave us.

'I claim the audacity to speak because I have survived life longer than anyone else here. You know that. I am in every honour society of this village. My adult sons, too, have won their honours. You know them. I am fully of this soil and have always been. We know why we are here. Anyone who does not know is worse than deaf.

'But we are not by ourselves. We have fathers who have gone before us, and children who are coming after us. We are all one in one with them, part of the same stream of people, undivided, and what we do here today, we must do in union with them. It is proper then that before we start, we consult our fathers and ask them to let us benefit from their wisdom. Community, agree with me!'

Agreed!

Kwenu!

Hey!

Kwenu!

Hey!

'All right then. Three of us, the oldest among us, but not by our own power, will go before our sacred shrines with the proper sacrifices. By your concordance, because the community is the community of all, those who know, and even those who do not know . . . We shall go and justify ourselves. It is said that whoever is on his way should not leave his brothers behind because travel is best in company . . .'

The three old men leave with sacrificial objects, four albino kola nuts, *oji ugo*, the rare one that is milky white instead of the usual red, four pods of alligator pepper, four fresh eggs. Father Higler follows them with his eyes as they walk towards the shrines. They are bare to their waists. Skins of wrinkled leather, complexions of a humus brown, as if they were scooped out of the very soil on which they stand – three savage priests at a Solemn High Mass – the sub-deacon, the deacon and the celebrant. They assist one another and trade responses. *Ogu's*. Psalmic incantations of justification. Reproaches to their fate. Exhortations to their gods. Their gods, inscrutable like all gods, are not exempt from obligation.

We ask to be spared.

Why should we be condemned without reprieve?

Why should our own gods treat us like strangers? . . .

Who is after me must run while I run.

The same rain that falls on the slave falls on the slave driver.

The disease that insists on seeing me to my grave must accompany me there.

All men are like fingers on the same hand. If one finger is smeared, all are smeared.

Who stands in the door to keep me from going through cannot go through himself.

A snake that swallows its mate ends up with a tail sticking out of its mouth.

Egbe bere!
Ugo bere,
Nke si ibe ya ebela,
Nku kwakwa ya!

Let the kite perch!
Let the eagle also have a perch,
Whichever begrudges the other a perch,
May he lose a wing.
Egbe bere!
Ugo bere,
Nke si ibe ya ebela,
Nanu ya bere!
– Whichever begrudges the other a perch
By himself let him perch!
The hunter does not aim at a bird in flight
When one is sitting smugly on a branch.
We do not know where we came from.
And who knows where we are going?
We cry when we are first born.
Others cry when we breathe our last.
Between the first and the last cry,
We do what we can.
The *nziza* (tiny bird) cannot bleed more blood than he's got.
He that wishes evil on his neighbours,
Let evil follow him.
He that wishes good,
Let the good be on his path.
We lay our hands on *Ofo*
We lay our hands on *Ogu*
Ogu bu nka (Justification begets longevity)
Ofo bu ike (Rightness is strength)
We are not on our own
A dead man cannot dig his own grave nor bury himself.
We belong to the land –
We are stuck on it!
Eat from it!
Drink from it!
Started from it!
End in it!
Unless we have knowingly done harm,
Why should we be harmed . . .?

The old men went on with their recitations as if all the time in God's eternity had been reserved for their pleasure, and while they lingered the rest of the assembly sated itself on casual talk. For his part, Father Higler found himself thinking first about their strange ceremonies but ultimately about the unusualness of his being there in their midst. This was the stuff of legends and travel lore, half-naked natives under a big tree going through strange, savage rituals. How did he get here? What was he doing here? What would be his future here? He began thinking of that first day when he had appeared among them a little over a year before, their sur-reality then, their even deeper surreality now, the apparent simplicity of their lives on casual observation, the underlying, almost intractable complexity.

The sky had been drenching fire that first day, the sun seemingly having abandoned its assigned perch millions of miles away and descended to a point just above the tree tops. From there it had spewed fire on everything, a big dripping ball of liquid metal. Such heat, he was told, was rather unseasonable, the worst of the heat was supposed to be over, but heat was never really unseasonable here. His throat had been parched, his mouth gummy, his ears humming. Rivulets of sweat ran down the sides of his face into his ears, down the valley of his back into the cleft of his buttocks.

There had been the endless, almost changeless green forest on either side of the roads and bypaths through which the bicycle taxi took him. Trees, bearded and tentacled, faking the shapes of monsters, a silent, brooding ubiquitous presence just off the corners of the eyes, sinister spirits tres-passing into reality when the face was turned elsewhere. A preserved replica of what the world might have been before the spirit of God passed over it.

And then there was the Imo River, the sight of which had made him thirstier than ever. But he had stood helpless by the bank unable to will himself to drink the dirty water, in and out of which waded fishermen, women washing clothes on some boulders, men and boys bathing naked. He could not ignore the warnings he had so pointedly received, the infinite list of tropical diseases in the air, water and soil, each waiting to make short shrift of his apostleship. So he had stood helplessly watching the cyclist as the man found a secluded spot for himself, washing his limbs and face, and, using his hands as cup, drank zestily out of the water. The river channel was about half a mile across, a slow procession of water – muddy dark-brown water like the faces and bodies of the people who waded and bathed in it, possessed of the same unfathomable mysteries.

And then there had been the arrival at Saint Peter Claver's, a solitary clearing, a mere tonsure on the head of the forest, marked by two large huts with mud walls and roofs of raffia thatch. Near the road a sign had been painted in green runny paint and nailed between two fence posts which had sprouted and grown into little trees. The inscription proclaimed that this was Saint Peter Claver's Roman Catholic Mission Church.

Just then, as now, he had found himself immersed in a sea of black faces and bodies, deep torpid eyes. Only then he could not understand what they were saying. Some parishioners had been awaiting his arrival. They made him welcome with their smiles. A few like Philip and Matthew who could speak some English came forward to express their joy at seeing him.

'We're all going to get along now, aren't we?' he said. 'And build a big parish here? A really big one? And spread the word of God, huh? Very well. Very well! Starting right tomorrow, huh? No time to waste.'

'Filipu. Me, I am Filipu. Your obedient servant. I cook for you.' A trace of a smile flitted across his face, but then was quickly gone again.

'Very well, very well, Philip. What's for supper tonight?'

More people arrived and he had been elated to see them and had waded enthusiastically into their midst, throwing hellos and pumping their hands. 'Are you baptized? . . . Do you go to Church? Are you a Christian?' Most of their answers were lost on him, just as most of his questions were lost on them, except when Philip or Matthew or Paul stepped up to interpret.

Then he had grown weary of it all, physically weary, as his body seemed suddenly to remember its tiredness. He had sat on the veranda of the rectory and they had stood just outside it and a silent vigil had ensued between him and them across an invisible chasm. For his part he had begun to look past them, past the clearing and the road to the elemental forest that surrounded everything, sweaty, solemn and inviolate, stretching southwards for miles past Aba from which he had just come, until it dissolved into the sordid, fever-ridden mangrove swamps, and finally into that part of the Gulf of Guinea which was called the Bight of Biafra.

Then, as now, he had wondered what he was doing here.

By sundown, cloud banks were churning like amorphous monsters trying to swallow one another. Lightning was rattling.

'It looks like a storm coming,' he had commented to Philip.

'Yes Fada.'

'I thought your rainy season was supposed to be over in September?'

'Yes Fada.'

'Then why is it threatening to rain now?'

Philip had shrugged his shoulders. Why should he have known, he seemed to say. A pause.

'Fada eat first or baff first?'

'Or what?' The servant's intonations needed getting used to.

'Baff. Wash body.' He made explanatory gestures.

'Oh bathe. I see. I'll bathe first.'

After the bath, Philip had served a peppery supper of rice and stewed chicken, and then enacted his household routines which were as unchanging as the ordinary of the mass. He ate in silence, periodically startled by flashes of lightning.

So this was the Africa he had dreamed about in the last few years, and had sought in his wildest imaginings to re-create mentally in the tame, hallowed and cloistered environs of Saint Mary's, surrounded by an imperially dignified and civilized English countryside, which countryside in comparison to Saint Mary's was considered a defiled 'outside world', kept at bay by high fences and wrought iron gates and invisible ramparts of divine grace. Even the air on Saint Mary's grounds seemed to be enriched by God's special beneficience, purified and blessed – an island of holiness and tranquillity. During the spring the flowers and shrubs grew as if they received from God more than the usual compliments of showers and sunshine. Blossoms were large, inflorescences spectacular. To come, to leap from those grounds to this pagan place where the very trees looked sinister and bedevilled! It was like getting a swimming lesson in a sterilized swimming pool and then being cast into a mire pit. There was no protection here, no wall or fence or outer defence perimeter. The jungle and the darkness and all that they represented stood close at hand, in the front of one's door.

'Fada want anything more?' Philip had asked, getting ready to depart.

He had thought for a moment. 'No, Philip. Nothing.'

'Yes Fada. I go now, but I come back in the morning early for mass.'

'Fine. Goodnight.'

'Yes Fada. Goodnight Fada.'

Philip had walked off into the thickening gloom in a pattern that later he repeated daily. His life had a light and dark side, one aspect known, another aspect hidden; days at the mission, nights among his own people.

Long after Philip had gone, Father Higler had stood in the front door above the veranda contemplating the darkness and the swords of lightning which slashed it. There was no moon and no stars – only an ominous ethereal glow underneath the convulsive clouds. A fresh wind arose, shocking the trees and shaking them into frantic submission. The crack and whooshing fall of a branch being snatched from one of the trees near the road. The winds changing directions, relenting, starting again and changing again. The trees dancing and shaking to the contradictory orders of a fickle god, and he standing in his place, watching, wincing, his soutane wrapped tightly around him while its edges snap at his feet like mad and angry puppies.

Then the rains had come, first in large heraldic drops which pelted the leaves and the ground and tattooed on the roof like pebbles on the face of a large, limp drum. And he had withdrawn into the parlour, locking the doors, and later in to his bedroom. The sounds of conflict outside had receded a little, though he could still hear the rattle and whipsnap of lightning and the boom of thunder and the tumultuous stampede of the rain attenuating at rare intervals to the sounds of bacon frying in a giant pan.

Sleep had fled from his eyes. His imagination had vaulted back and forth across ages and times, oceans and continents, moods of frolicking in blessed sunshine to languishing in cursed and satanic tempests. He had probed the ocean of solitude around him, weighed himself against its enormousness. On a prompting he had got out of bed again and forced open the lone window of his bedroom, and at once the wind had snatched it and flattened it against the wall, out of reach, and he had been confronted by the driven rain and all the darkness he could wish to see – thick, black, unshaded and undifferentiated darkness, washed by fierce, unseen raindrops, fanned by capricious, unseen gales. There had seemed to be something out there scowling at him, and he had been unable to close the window against the wind and had dreaded that at any moment a fatal dart might hit him in the face from that outer darkness.

But by and by the storm had waned. The winds had retired and the rains had calmed to a steady, non-turbulent pour, and finally to a drizzle.

A knock at the door. Lamp in hand, fearful but without choice, he had gone to investigate. A muffled voice had issued out of the darkness.

'Who is it?' he had asked.

'Filipu.'

'Philip!' His voice was between exclamation and question.

'Yes Fada,' came the servant's signatory answer.

'Well, what are you doing out there? Come out of the darkness.'

Philip emerged from the darkness wet from the rain, clad only in an old pair of shorts. 'Fada, I did not want my wetness to spoil the floor.' He shook the rain off the banana leaf which had ill-served him as an umbrella.

'What brings you out at this ungodly hour?'

'Fada, I came to see if Fada was all right. How Fada manage in the rain.'

'H'm. You want to come inside? Come in.'

'Yes Fada.'

'Come on. It looks like you're wet all through.' They entered the parlour. 'That was quite a storm.'

'Yes Fada.'

'Have a seat. And thanks for your concern. Go on and sit in the chair.'

But Philip sat on the floor under the lamp which hung from a nail in the wall, his back arched into the nook where the two walls met, his knees drawn up, his hands draped over them.

'You were not afraid walking here alone in the dark? How far is it to where you live?'

'Fada, about half mile.'

'You walked that distance in this weather just to see how I was?'

Fada, the road is safe. The darkness is empty. There is nothing in it.'

He had weighed the statement briefly and wagged his head. 'I must say you are a very brave man.'

'I go now Fada, as Fada is all right. Or Fada want me to make a little tea for him?' He hoisted himself up.

'As a matter of fact I wouldn't mind some tea, if it is not too much trouble. Can you start a fire easily enough?'

'Yes Fada.'

A short time later Philip had a merry fire going and a kettle singing on it. He was seated on a low stool, stoking the embers frequently, tending them with the deft movements of a master craftsman, staring into the dancing flames as if he would be quite content to spend the rest of his life just watching them. Father Higler had found Philip strange that first night, and even stranger since then, strange beyond the strangeness he had noted in everything that was of this place.

Tea served. Philip had declined his offer to join him, meekly but unflinchingly, and returned to his nook and sat down, watching him as he poured the tea, dropped two cubes of sugar into the cup, stirred, and raised the cup to his mouth, while the steam rose over his face as if his beard were on fire.

'Good tea,' he had commented.

'Yes Fada,' Philip replied.

'Suppose you tell me a few things about our church and about the parishioners.'

'What Fada wish to know?'

'Just general things for my information. Why don't you begin with yourself?'

A smile seemed to tug at his lips, but if so it didn't pull them very far or for very long. He shrugged his shoulders and said: 'Me Fada, I am just Philip.' He shrugged his shoulders again. 'Nothing else.'

'Are you married?'

'No Fada.'

'H'm.' A sip of tea. Then he said: 'What about the other members of the church?'

Philip proceeded to name them – Paul, Matthew, Mark, Genesis, John, Mary. There were no stories, no dossiers, no backgrounds, just plain, unclothed names.

'What about Father Schlotz? What really happened to him?' He had not met his predecessor in Europe.

Philip shrugged his shoulders to that.

'And what does that signify?'

'Fada, he was sick.'

'I guessed as much. But what type of sickness? What really happened to him? Was it true that his mind went bad?'

'Fada, he was plenty sick. At first fever. Then it got bad. Very bad, Fada. All the medicine in the house gone. And still he is sick.'

'Go on . . .'

'Yes Fada. Now Fada, this is not what I say. It is what the village people say. And some of our church people too. They say the fever enter his head.' He tapped his skull with a fat, knobby finger. 'Me, all I know is that he began to refuse his chop, afternoon chop, night chop, until he is thin like a broomstick. Nobody know of anything to do. Then the fever make like it is gone. Then it comes back. Then it begin to come and go, to come and go. All the time, Fada's head less and less correct. Everybody is whispering. One day he leave mass in the middle and come back here in the house, and then he tear all of his clothes off . . . That one seemed to pass. And then all of his skin turn red and begin to come off like a lion scratched him. Then he began to shout in his sleep. The Committee people say I stay here with him at night. Of a sudden in the middle of the night he begin to shout out that something is scratching him and flogging him with whip. Then in the daytime too, he begin to see things . . .'

'H'm . . .' was all that Father Higler could say to this wild tale. If it were not the middle of the night, if he did not have a memory of the darkness from a short time earlier, he would have scoffed at the story. Of course he didn't believe it, but then again he did not feel inclined to ridicule it.

Philip went to the kitchen. When he returned, Father Higler had a question: 'Father Schlotz never saw a doctor at Aba?'

'Fada, I do not know. But he really got bad.'

'Aha,' the priest said. 'But tell me, what do you really mean by he was seeing things? Did he say so himself?'

'Yes, Fada. He said he saw them, but I do not know what he saw. Me I saw nothing.'

'H'm. You have no idea what really was the matter?'

Philip made as if to say something, then checked himself.

'What is it, Philip? What are you holding back?'

'It is nothing, Fada.' Then he stopped and seemed to think and then seemed to wish to revise his statement. 'But perhaps,' he started, 'since Fada has just come I will tell him.'

He proceeded with his eternal passivity. His face had an aspect of the darkness outside. It was there, deep and uniform, but most importantly there. Anyone beholding it had to take from it whatever pleased his own heart, but not at its suggestion. The eyes were unaccented solid gel. The voice was even and uninflected. 'Fada understand,' he was saying, scratching his chin, 'that this is not me speaking, but the village people who do not go to our church. And some of our church people also. They said it was the Land, *Mgbarala*, that was flogging him in his sleep and making his head not to be correct, that *Ala* has many different ways of getting people.'

'Nonsense!' sailed out of the priest's mouth. Then he was forced to chuckle at the simplicity of the superstition. It was so thoroughly absurd that no one should even be in danger of believing it.

'Fada, that was what they were saying.'

'You don't happen to believe that, do you?'

'Fada knows that I am a Christian. But Fada . . .' He paused and looked up at the priest. When the latter looked at him he lowered his eyes. 'Fada, there are some things that are hard to explain.'

'Nonsense!' he said again, seeming a little more serious now than when he first uttered the word a few moments before.

Philip sat unchanged, unflinching, his gaze steadily aimed to the floor at the priest's feet, his composure just as it would have been had the priest said: 'God bless you, brother.'

He had drained the last of his tea and set the cup firmly in the saucer, face down, and Philip had risen to clear the table. He had sat there watching the servant, pondering what he had related, allowing his imagination to devise the wildest conditions under which it could all make sense. There were none. But then he had reminded himself that this was Africa, a continent not necessarily on the same order of logic as he was used to, perhaps not even under the same eternal government. But that was the fault he had come to rectify. They that dwelt in darkness had to see the great light.

Philip had returned to the parlour and asked, 'Fada want anything more?'

'No,' he replied. 'Thank you very much, Philip, for the tea and for worrying about me.'

'Fada, I go now.'

'Why don't you stay here? What's the point walking half a mile back in this darkness when you will be here early in the morning?'

'Fada, the rain has stopped now. And there is nothing in the darkness.'

'Okay,' he had said, with genuine regret. 'Go in peace then.'

'Yes Fada.'

He had risen behind Philip, lamp in hand, and had stood in the veranda holding the lamp aloft. But he had succeeded only in lighting an island around himself, not the servant's path. Philip had stridden into the darkness, and the darkness had totally absorbed him back . . .

The three old men returned from their rites of justification. The din quieted. *Ofo* sticks made their way out of the raffia bags, short, stout, black sticks, mark of the priestly set. Fresh jugs of palm wine were emptied into the large open calabashes. Each *Ofo* holder rose, approached the calabashes, and washed his stick in the wine to the accompaniment of a short litany of incantations. After the washings, the drinking resumed – drinking the *Ofo* – the sacred community wine which united and beswore every participator to justice and fraternity.

Philip approached Father Higler for guidance. Should he, should the faithful, drink the pagan wine?

'No!' Father Higler answered.

A tumult arose.

They will not drink with us?

What is this we are seeing and hearing?

Who is saying they will not?

And why should they not if they are the true sons of this land?

Will they not commit themselves to the truth which justifies us to our gods and to our fathers who have been recalled from this life?

Then we must expel them from our concord, exclude them from our deliberations.

We do not exclude; they have excluded themselves.

Wait, their White Man is raising his hand to speak.

Speak, White Man!

Father Higler rose to defend the faith and the faithful. No offence was intended, but his followers could not swear themselves in this method.

He was interrupted. Which method then?

A smile. He continued. The faithful had wisely and bravely renounced the old pagan ways and received a new gift of faith from the one and only true God.

One true God?

Which god is true?

Our own gods are false, then?

The dare! He insults us. All of us!

The ground you are walking on, is it false, White Man?

And these trees, are they false?

The rains and the rivers, the yams in the farms!

The only falsehood issues from the mouths of men, and that is why we swear ourselves to the truth.

Look about you, White Man, pinch yourself. Is the pain false?

Show us the power of this true God!

Father Higler attempted several times to continue, but loud protests continually interrupted him. He was helpless, red in the face, sweaty and bristling at the beard. But at length the *ogele* sounded several times and restored the quiet.

It was not his place, Father Higler then went on, to judge or even guess how well their old gods had served them. All he knew was that there was a new order of things – not a new god, but an eternal and timeless God newly revealed. To make that God manifest among them was the reason he had journeyed into their midst the year before. To help them emerge from darkness into the light of God's grace and salvation. He invited them to join his faithful for now that the word had been given to them, their ignorance was no longer exempt from blame.

Ignorance! He is calling us fools!

A mere refugee among us!

Throw him out!

Withdraw our welcome and send him home!

Burn down his church.

Light a fire in his grisly beard.

Enough insult to kill him for.

The D. O. will never find him.

The dissension this time raged out of control. All efforts by Ahamba and the other old men to restore order failed. Loud arguments swirled around various spots where church members were situated.

Kill them all.

Ostracize them.

Read them out of our communion.

Burn down their houses, and sell them!

But at long last, quiet did return. 'Let us cool our tempers,' Ahamba said, 'and not forget why we are here in the first place.'

'I am sorry for all this,' Father Higler interjected. 'I intended no offence.'

'He is speaking again!'

'Be sorry, White Man! but hold your tongue. You have already spoken enough!' Ahamba's voice was fiercely strident.

'Now,' the old man continued, 'the elders of the eight compounds of this village will go out and confer among us.'

A short confab, a little distance away, and then the elders returned.

Did the priest not believe in the truth?

He did.

Did he not believe in swearing to the truth?

He did.

Was there nothing sacred to him, something, potent also, that he and his followers could swear on?

There was. The Holy Bible.

Was it really potent?

Yes. Most potent. Frightfully potent. He sought to impress them that God – the singular and true one he served, was even more wrathful and vindictive than all of theirs.

In that case then, they were willing to let him and his followers swear on this book of theirs.

Philip went to fetch it, brought back the Roman Missal instead of the Bible. No matter. A holy book was a holy book. The missal with its size, black and red print, thumb indentations and many-coloured markers, looked impressive enough. But the elders of the village, for their own good but unrevealed reasons, insisted on a method of swearing which inculcated communion and consumption, something that oath takers could ingest, drink, eat and swallow, whereby the hook of truth was buried in them.

How to obtain the right mixture of rituals?

Matthew remembered having seen a salting ceremony on a Bible. He explained. The method seemed worthy of trial, and so grains of salt were spread across the open pages of the missal, and the faithful, stepping forward, made the Sign of the Cross on themselves and licked grains of salt off the face of the holy book. At length they were all sworn.

Then the decision of the elders was announced. Father Higler was to be excluded from the rest of their deliberations!

All his appeals denied, the priest rose to take his leave, feeling neither outraged nor humiliated. He had come in peace, and besides he had no power to compel his wishes on them, no will, in fact, even if such power had been available to him. They had a right to their peace, without him as with him. That is, if they had peace. But they thought they did, and was the thought itself not as good as the reality? Ignorance. Bliss. He could not overwhelm them, there was nothing with which to overwhelm them, no visible signs, no compelling examples. He had to urge and nudge them forward. But what with? The promise of life after death seemed very remote to them. They were a sensual people. Their gods were immediate and direct, elected, and it seemed, disposable. He would have to make his inroads through their weak points, the poor and perhaps the children – the children especially, so that in ten or twenty years they would have grown up knowing the faith, in the faith, and perhaps keeping the faith.

In front of the mission clearing he ran into a group of children, faithless ones, for he could not remember seeing any of them at catechism classes.

'Good day,' he called out cheerfully.

'Goo day! Goo day,' they replied in turn, each sampling the new expression.

'*Ndewo nu*,' he added.

'*Ndewo*,' they replied and giggled among themselves.

They bombarded him with questions:

How did he lose all his colour and become so white?

By going to church every day, he answered facetiously.

How did he get his beard to grow so long?

By saying his prayers every night.

Really? Anybody who said prayers, would he grow a beard as long as his?

They should try it and see.

Even if the person were only a child?

They ought to try it and see. But first they had to come to catechism classes when they heard the gong in the evenings so he could teach them how to say the right prayers. Were they coming? Hands up those who will come tomorrow.

Two doubtful hands.

But they crowded around him, squatting and kneeling and offered to remove scores of prickly seeds which had attached themselves to his soutane when he had wandered off the footpath.

Would his beard grow some day to touch his knees?

Did he use his moustache to filter his drinks?

When he ate was he not afraid that some of the beard would enter his mouth and be chewed up with his food?

What was inside the big book he was holding?

Did it have any pictures?

They were interesting; they were refreshing; they were children – children of the new day – out of the pitch darkness and into the twilight, destined some day to emerge, if it pleased God, into the full blessedness of the sunshine of God's faith. They represented a hope.

6

Later that afternoon. Philip returned to the mission as if all hope had deserted him. The deep eyes underneath their heavy folds and the characteristically expressionless face bore the marks of great concern.

'Well, Philip,' said Father Higler, looking up from his reading on the veranda. 'How did the rest of the deliberations go?'

Philip shrugged. 'They just end, Fada.'

'How did they end? What was said after I left?'

'Fada, they said I was the one who caused the death of John. They put everything on me.'

'Rubbish! How could they reach a conclusion like that? You did not start the fights, nor did you bring the gun. So of all people involved how could you be singled out for blame?'

'Fada, they said it was my finger which made the gun go off.'

'Even worse rubbish! How could they possibly establish whose finger was on the trigger? Who saw it? You were trying to prevent the other fellow from using the gun.'

'Fada, they went to the seers. They consulted two seers, and both of them said me.'

Father Higler snapped his breviary shut in a surge of anger. 'Is that the basis on which they have condemned you? A seer's oracle?'

'Yes Fada.'

'Nonsense. Bunkum! Pay no heed to any of it. What of the other fellow? What did they blame him for?'

'For bringing the gun, Fada. They said he brought the gun but he did not shoot it.'

'He should have been blamed for the entire episode. He introduced the weapon, and apparently meant to use it. Even if while trying to retrieve it from him your hand had brushed across the trigger, that doesn't make you guilty of anything. It would have to be considered an accident.'

'Even if it was an accident, Fada, the blood of the dead is still on my head.'

'No, it is not.'

'Yes Fada, it is!'

Father Higler looked up at Philip insisting on his own guilt. Exhaling, he asked: 'Was any punishment assessed against you? Are you required to do anything?'

'Fada, they said, they said – Fada, they said I should make sacrifices of atonement to the Land and wash my hands of the blood that was spilled.'

'Sacrifices, huh?' Father Higler was caught between a sigh and a chuckle. He chuckled first, then sighed. 'Was that all? Is that all they asked you to do?'

'Yes Fada.'

'You will assist me at mass in the morning. That is going to have to be enough sacrifice for them. And you can drop into the chapel and say a few Hail Marys for John's soul.'

But Philip gave no appearance of being relieved. He did not say the customary 'Yes Fada' and he did not go away. Rather he hung around as if he craved further comforting.

'I am quite hungry, Philip.'

'Yes Fada.' He breathed hard. 'But Fada, what really am I to do?'

'Nothing, Philip. You don't have to do anything. They did not say you had to participate in some kind of public ceremony, did they?'

'No Fada. They have nothing to do with it now. It is now between me and the Land.'

'Fine then. Just ignore the whole thing. I'm sure the Land, whatever it is, will show better understanding than your fellow villagers.'

'God will protect me, Fada?'

'Yes, of course, God will protect you. But in the first place, I don't see what there is to protect you against. You are perfectly safe.'

'I believe you, Fada.'

'It is not a matter of believing me, but of sheer common sense which realizes the impotence of all the idols. And then having faith in God.'

'Fada knows God, and Fada is a man of God. I know if you promise that God will protect me, he will.'

'Mmmmh,' Father Higler grunted at the imputation of such close liaison between him and God. 'Just maintain your faith, Philip,' he said, 'and say your prayers regularly.'

'And I can ignore making the sacrifices?'

'The sacrifices are out of the question, Philip, if you want to remain a Christian. You were not thinking of making them, were you?' He looked up alertly.

Philip bit his lips. 'No Fada.' He sighed, exhaled. 'I see Fada never in doubt before.'

'Yes, Philip, I have been in doubt before. Of course, I have. We all have our doubts at one time or another. But the mere doubt, the temptation itself is not a sin. The important thing is not to yield to our doubts. You might recall that even Our Lord himself at one desperate moment on the cross cried out: "My God, my God, why hast thou forsaken me!" The important thing is to emerge from such situations of doubt with a fresh reassurance, a renewal of our faith . . .'

For Philip, however, the dead tree gave no shelter, and the dry stone no sound of water. 'What,' he asked, 'would Fada do if Fada was me?'

Father Higler swallowed. That was an impossible proposition, and to wit an unkind one. He had enough trouble being just himself, bearing his own sweet yoke, wrestling with his own eternal fate, without being asked to assume responsibility for another's. But he was a priest, and it was his duty to try. He sighed.

'Nothing, Philip,' he answered. 'I would do absolutely nothing. What is there to do but have faith in God. And hope.'

60

Philip swallowed heavily and grunted 'Mmmmh.' The leap of faith was across an abyss with no knowledge of how far the other side was – if the other side was there at all. One leaped and hoped for a landing, a soft and happy landing.

So Philip went away to do the priest's cooking. That day passed. Others came and went. Catechism. More frequent choir practices now that Christmas was drawing nearer. The masons came from time to time and installed a few dozen bricks around the perimeter of the new church, raising the height on some of the walls. Moulded a few new bricks as the cement was available. Father Higler continued to visit the local market on the days it was in session, and to make his forays into the throngs of the still faithless and to urge the faith on them. They listened patiently, joked about his gallantry in attacking the language. Some enjoyed bandying words with him, others pressed gifts on him. He had some successes, but no sudden floods of God's faith overwhelmed this village or the nearby ones into which he journeyed from time to time.

Philip – Oh Philip. Thought of the servant would sometimes obtrude into his mind and so arrest it that he would stop whatever he was doing. He would wonder about the servant's plight.

Have we, Oh Lord, not forsaken everything and followed thee?

Philip was clearly in distress. A marked man by his own reckoning and apparently the reckoning of the rest of the village, including his fellow parishioners. He stalked about like a man afflicted with an irremediably fatal disease, a man expecting a certain ambush from some unknown quarter. And his fellow villagers eyed him as if any hour, any minute, the Land, the remorseless god with whom he had been trifling, would come to grips with him and snuff him out.

'Fada what do I do? What I can do?'

The servant's plea echoed again and again in his heart. And so did his own helpless answer. 'Nothing, Philip. Nothing. Nothing need be done. There is nothing to do. Nothing *can* be done . . .'

'Listen, White Man . . .'

Old man Ahamba was always asking him to look or to listen, standing where he always stood by the flower beds in front of the veranda, and for some reason known only to him, never entering the rectory.

'He is of this soil, this soil here!' Stamping his foot and his long walking stick on the ground. 'There is no escape. Not even in death are we free and disobliged. No, our union with it thickens even then. You know, when a child is delivered before it is washed and taken out to be shown, the afterbirth must first be buried in the soil. And four days later when the stalk of the umbilical cord falls off, we bury it also in the soil, and plant a young tree over it. The tree grows with the child . . . You see, there is no difference between us and the Land of our origin, no separation. If one of us has the misfortune to die in a foreign soil we send a delegation that may have to travel many days and nights to bring him back, so that he may be re-united . . . So I say to you, White Man, these people in your church now, they are like birds that have left their nests in a tree. They may fly all day long, but they must come back to the tree. Even you, White Man, are now of us. You did not start here, but you are here now. You have eaten the fruits of this Land; it has sunk its hooks in you. So even you cannot totally escape . . .'

Father Higler interrupted the monologue with a chuckle. 'I too must now pay obeisance to the Land?'

'As long as you live here. You may have your own god where you come from, or up in the sky as you say. But you are here now, not there. And if you should be besieged here, can your god so far away reach down here and rescue you? . . . We know there is D. O. at Aba. He can come here with his soldiers and police, but if we decided to do something to you, can the D. O. save you? How long would it take him to come here? You would be many days dead then. That is the way it is with your God. Remember the other man who came before you, how it was his head lost its correctness in the middle of one afternoon? . . . I tell you it takes caution to survive here. Alertness. Looking around. But you, you are a stranger who will some day return to your own place. It is those that are from here, the native sons of this soil, who must look behind them. What kills a tree often comes from its roots and not its branches. So especially for your pot boiler, he must look behind him to his roots . . . As for yourself, remember that we were here before you came – we gave the one who came before you this place to stay. We even helped him to clear the bush and build this very house where you now live. If you want more land or to push the bush back, ask us. We will probably say yes to whatever you request – we have a saying that there is always enough land for the dead man to have the size of grave he desires . . . We ourselves never clear the bush or build without asking the gods and spirits of the place. It is a deference to things bigger than ourselves. And as I say, caution helps longevity.'

'Yes Ahamba,' Father Higler replied. 'I appreciate your concern for me, but mine is really for Philip.'

'Your pot boiler. Well, he has fled to refuge with you. Can you protect him? As you live here among us, if someone from another village molested you, we would be ready to go to war to save you. Is your pot boiler safe with you? What do you offer him for the risk you have asked him to take?'

'Philip is safe enough if your jujus are all he has to worry about. Nobody is going to do him any physical harm and blame it on the jujus, are they?'

'Mmmmh, my friend. If he offends us, the people, he pays to us. If he has offended the Land, it is between him and the Land.'

'Fine. Let it be between him and the Land then. I am told you based your determination on the words of an oracle.'

'The seer who cannot see saw it for us. The blind one who is famous in all the villages around here. Him and also another.'

'But that is preposterous. How can a man of your intelligence, experience and wisdom fall victim to such chicanery?'

'As you like, White Man. As you like. But chicanery? You who would convince me that a woman conceived without knowing a man? That a dead man buried for three days – he should have started rotting by then – rose again from the dead, spread his wings and flew into heaven? Ah, my friend, beliefs are like wives, each man chooses as it pleases him.'

'Would you stake your life on what that deceitful seer said?'

'Deceitful? How can I call him deceitful unless I have been given the truth myself, which I am not. Akhee-khee-khee. Would I stake my life on the seer's truth? Akhee-khee . . . I would ask the seer to stake his life first, since it is his truth, to try his neck in the noose first. Akhee-khee . . .'

'Which means you really do not seriously believe any of these things.'

'Mind your own beliefs, White Man, and your own gods. Mine have learned to understand me.'

'Understand you?'

'Yes, I insist on it.'

'The nerve!'

'At my age I can. I have learned to bargain.'

'Bargain, my friend! How do you dare?'

'But I do dare. Fear, White Man, fear. Our fears are older than our beliefs. When our fears die down, our beliefs change. But tell me, do you have any doubts about your beliefs?'

'No. My faith in God, by God's own grace, remains unshakable.'

'If you were younger, I would say it was your youth.'

'Age has nothing to do with it.'

'Then you are lying. Or you are very strange.'

'Neither, my good old friend. I am neither lying nor strange. You've just never been gifted with faith. It is a wonderful feeling – the evidence of things which appear not.'

'Still you would not believe a seer?'

'Not a mere old rogue and trickster – even when he is blind.'

'We all have preferences about whom to be tricked by.'

'I have not been tricked. You have. You and the entire village.'

'Stay well, my friend. I leave you now. But look about you. And do not forget what I always told you. All gods are a little mad, and if you wish to serve them right, it is good to be a little drunk yourself . . .'

'Fare thee well, my good friend. Come and see me again soon. I might yet make a good Christian out of you.'

'Mmmmh,' Old Ahamba grunted, showed his back and walked away.

The season advanced. The harmattan blew harder and colder. Dust rose in wild swirls and then settled on the vegetation like a brown coat. Lips cracked; skins scaled. Father Higler's flowers died in spite of frequent watering and his other attentive care, the balsams first, then the zinnias. The canna lily produced large clusters of stunted shoots with no buds.

Father Schlotz had introduced here a Harvest Thanksgiving Festival, a moveable feast, which gave the faithful an alternative to the pagan *Ihe Ala*, the grand feast of *Mgbarala*, the premier juju of the entire village. Harvest was also good for morale and for funds. The villagers, Christian and non-Christian, doted on ceremonies. Benediction and sung masses attracted large audiences, for the burning and shaking of incense, the raising of the monstrance, the sprinkling of holy water, the undulating songs. The choir shouted itself hoarse at high masses, chasing Latin hymns up and down gravelly hills and valleys. And with the choir groping ahead, in search of the tune, the congregation followed jauntily and spiritedly, especially with the more common songs like the Kyrie, Gloria or the Credo, imposing meaningless sounds for the Latin words they did not understand.

Harvest this year was scheduled for the Fourth Sunday in Advent, just four days before Christmas. In the week before the parishioners gifted the church – or God – with their proverbial ewes and fatted calves, products from their farms – yams, cocoyams, melons, palm fruit, corn, fluted pumpkins, cassava, coconuts and handicrafts – all displayed in a heap at the back of the church for God's glory and the satisfaction of the givers.

The mission grounds were cleaned and decorated. Early in the week the boys weeded the paths, mowed the lawns, put a new fence around the back of the rectory and Philip's kitchen, and new raffia mats on the roof of the old church. The women cleaned the interior of the church, and rubbed a fresh coat of clay on the walls, floor and pews. The pews were narrow earthen mounds which looked like elongated coffins, raised about two feet above the floor. Later in the week, the altar table was oiled and polished. The interior of the church was decked and festooned with leafy boughs and shrubs. Palm fronds were woven into intricate patterns and arched around doors and windows.

And then the big Sunday came, and the parishioners showed up bedecked in their gaudiest finery. Everyone who had the least smattering of faith was in the congregation that morning, and many who had never come before chose that day to make their start. They came and they all came late to ensure that everyone saw what they were wearing.

Mass this morning was only a side attraction, and so was quickly disposed of. Father Higler preached a sermon based on the day's *Introit*:

Drop down the dew, ye heavens, from above;
And let the clouds rain the just.
Let the earth be opened
And bud forth the Saviour.

He talked to them about the dew that was falling outside, about the harmattan which whittled and killed things, but how God nevertheless kept them alive with the dew, and how early in the coming year the first rains would revive the thirsty vegetation. That, he said, was like the coming of Christ, the Saviour, to water the moribund and thirsty hearts of men. He urged them to be ready, to prepare their hearts as they would prepare their homes, for the coming of a great man.

At the end of the mass came the monetary donations. Processions of gift givers marched to the altar where the receptacles were displayed in front of Father Higler and Philip, who sat in their white and black vestments and among the busy decorations like two strange gods receiving the sacrifices of their anxious worshippers. One was diminutive, white, freckled, almost bald, heavily bearded and lost in his voluminous robes. The other was sturdy, black, saturine-faced and uncomfortably stuffed in his undersized raiment. One shifted in his seat often, and from time to time a smile broke through his beard when his eyes met those of the gift-givers. The other sat almost unmoving, his face serenely morose, as if he found being a god a tedious task foisted on him against his will making him indifferent to the halo and the glory. The palm branches waved around them. The candles danced at their backs.

In front of them, behind a table, Matthew stood as mediator between them and the congregation, a combination of priest and auctioneer, exhorting the people to virtue and loosehandedness, receiving their sacrifices and dispensing to them the blessings of the gods. 'Give!' he urged them. 'Give from the bottom of your heart! Give to God with an open hand and he too will give back to you with an open hand! Remember what it says in the Bible: "I shall reward every gift a hundred fold." Christian mothers, come and give your gifts to God!' Matthew intoned in his most eloquent cadences, and the hefty matrons of Christianity in that otherwise heathen land hoisted themselves up from their seats and dribbled forward in swaddling wrappers to throw their manilas, half-pennies and cowries into the collection plate at the altar.

'Collected by the Christian mothers,' Matthew shouted, 'two shilling two pence 'apenny! Clap for them!' There was a big applause, led by the Christian mothers themselves.

'And now,' Matthew said, 'if the women collected so much, let us see how many times over the men will double it. Let us see. Let us see. Christian fathers, are you present here, or are you hiding? Let us see you bring your gifts to God!'

They that had been called marched to the altar with their donations.

'The Christian fathers gave . . .' Matthew announced. 'Now, does that not mean we should give them a very big, big clap. I say, clap for them!'

A round of clapping.

'Now the Christian mothers say they are annoyed. They say they want to show the men something. They will come back to the altar with more gifts. Let us see how the men will take that challenge from the women . . .'

'Men will always be men. The Christian fathers say that since the women have insulted them by going to the altar for the second time and daring to come near to them in contribution, they too will come again to the altar and show these women how and why it is that God made Adam first and used only *one* of his ribs to make Eve . . .'

The contributions went on and on this way. People took donations to the altar as Matthew continued to classify them. The rest of the congregation clapped endlessly. The ushers whose task it was to count the money stayed busy.

'Now the young men . . .

'Clap for them . . .

'Now the young women . . .

'Clap for them . . .

'Those who feel that God did something for them in this year that is now passing . . .

'Clap for them . . .

'Now those who would like God to do something for them in this year that will soon come . . .

'Clap for them . . .'

Clap! Clap! Clap!

Three days later it was Christmas Eve. Matthew once again eagerly took over the direction of the activities, and as usual with great success. All the magic it took was a big bonfire near the masons' shed, two drums to start with, and a group of children eager to sing. The fire was lit shortly after dark, and the boys were only too glad to keep it going with twigs and broken branches. Then they started chanting and singing and beating drums. These attracted more people.

Matthew then suggested that they go carolling before the midnight mass. After some initial misgivings Father Higler said 'Why not?' They divided into two groups. One went carolling and the other stayed behind at the mission, singing, beating the drums and dancing around the big fire.

Philip had gone carolling, and so at eleven Father Higler went to where the tom-tom lay under the mango tree and began sounding it. The sounds exploded loudly in his ears, and then fled with their message into the surrounding forests, there to echo and reverberate like thunder trapped in a bottle. Finally he put away the beater and straightened up to notice the full moon looming up behind the trees in the low horizon, ascending slowly like a delicate, white balloon, inflated with haze and precariously suspended on thin, blue mist.

Walking back to the fire, he found that the boys had stopped their singing for a moment and were arguing good-humouredly about what song to sing next and whose turn it was next to beat the drums. He wandered away from their fire and their voices to the outer fringes of the mission which sat in shadows and apparent tranquillity. Shadows. The moon seemed to create more shadows than it dispersed. In the semi-darkness, the poorly-illumined vegetation stood in its own badly etched shadows to produce a continuous half-shadow.

He paced around like a bearded ghost, flashlight in hand, arms folded across his chest against the relative cold. This was Africa, he thought. Africa. The azure sky enamelled in places with white clouds, the shadows, the dancing flames, the crackling wood, the hoarse and discordant singing of the boys around the fire, the echoes of the carollers some distance away. Saints in the wilderness.

He thought of his arrival here the year before, late in October, the Tuesday after the feast of Christ the King, three days before the feast of All Saints. He recalled the large congregation that had turned out to make the acquaintance of the new priest that first Sunday. Because of the heavy storm the day of his arrival the Epistle he had read to them had seemed most appropriate:

"Do not harm the earth or the sea or the trees till we have sealed the servants of our God on their foreheads!"

The 'tribes', the 'tongues', the 'multitudes which no one could number, standing before the throne and before the Lamb, clothed in white robes and with palms in their hands'.

Memories mixed with desires.

After mass that day he had called Philip. 'Come here, Philip.'

'Yes Fada.'

'You have to teach me to speak Igbo.'

'Yes Fada.'

'What's the word for "come"?'

'*Bia. Bia.*'

'*Bia.*'

'Good. Fada learn already. Fada learn quick like the other Fada.'

'Father Schlotz? How did he get along with the language?'

'Fada I teach him and before the word is out of my mouth he already learned.'

'What is the word for "church"?'

'*Uka.*'

'*Bia uka!*'

'Yes Fada. That is very good Fada.' Philip had clapped his hands in applause.

Then there had been his pledge to visit every compound in the village and make friends. That pledge was fulfilled. To build a stone church. Ah . . . When that thought had first come to him it had so arrested him that he slapped his breviary shut, and stood motionless to savour it. Yes, a stone church! It had brought a smile to his lips. A cathedral of classic splendour with high flung arches and stained windows right here in the middle of the jungle. After a year an unfulfilled hope, stunted by its own size. There was then the bell – ah yes – at least that was on its way, thanks to the kindness of his friends in England. But the ultimate hope, the hope to which all others were the tributaries – the conversion of multitudes of villagers – that was still unfulfilled. Deferred. Re-deferred.

He was suffused with indefinable feelings as he ambled by the edges of the forest, mindless of the danger of snakes, a ghostly shadow in the moonlight. His heart was teased by a nostalgia for precious things irrecoverably lost, things vague and elusive, amorphous and impalpable, yet managing to engender inarguable feelings of loss – alloyed memories falsified by unrequited desires, counterfeits gilded in imitation and alchemic gold, suggesting pleasures never enjoyed and golden ages never lived.

Why are all our golden ages behind us? Was there ever a time far away and long ago, when our smiles lasted longer than our sighs and our tears succumbed to laughter?

Clare.

No! No, not Clare! Not now! An hour before Christmas mass. He would not think of her. He would forget her, banish thoughts of her. At least for now.

Clare. She sat on a mound and pretended to be smoking a dried twig, looking at him talk. A girl of his youth. But she was not a girl now, just as he was not a youth now – a woman a few years younger than he was. How many years since? . . . It had been a long life with erratic turns. The haunting distance of those days before he joined the army, the walk in the woods in the late spring. Illicit privileges. Unlicensed and damnable actions. Straddling flesh and spirit, shuttling between the dictates of nature and those of nature's God. The celebration of love. Fear. The promises of the imagination and the disappointments of the flesh. Shame.

'Anton, you will come back to me?'

'Of course, darling.'

Of course . . .

The midnight mass was in the open, in the full face of the night and the forest, under the gaze of the bleary-eyed moon. The mist descended from the sky like divine grace; the flames of the bonfire leaped sprightly into the night, fed periodically from a heap of dried branches and twigs by a group of people who surrounded it for warmth. Elsewhere the mission was dotted with a myriad of lights – a few hurricane lamps of European make, scores of *owa* torches made of split raffia bamboo, faggots tied together, wood torches dipped periodically in pools of wax held in coconut shells, lanterns made from tin containers to which nozzles had been attached to hold a wick. Each had its own character; they all shed their lights – dim, bright or smoky – around their holders, who sat, squatted or knelt on the ground, eyes turned to the altar where Father Higler and Philip, enshrined

69

in a halo of several candles, were muttering or chanting strange prayers into the night.

It seemed that the whole village, Christian and pagan alike, had turned out for the ceremony, a high mass which Father Higler sang with fervour. At the end he preached the Christmas message to them. The word had now gone out from God, he declared, that all the people of his kingdom be counted. Just as in Caesar's time. That explained his presence among them. He was like a census taker, but it was up to them to see that their names were entered into the Book of Life and kept there. And they should be willing to take as much trouble as Mary and Joseph had taken to ensure that their names were registered.

When mass was over, a group led by Matthew wanted to go carolling again. Father Higler let them have their wish, and went to bed himself. Their singing woke him up some hours later, and once or twice still later he heard their distant voices proclaiming the message of Christ's coming to the rest of their heathen village. They carolled all night, until the cold moonlight dissolved into the bright light of dawn. He was glad they were his people.

A bazaar was held two days later, and with great success. The people came and bought back their own gifts for cash.

Days passed. The harmattan became more severe. Attendance at the catechism classes and at morning mass fell. He and Philip would often sit in their vestments in prayerful silence waiting for the first parishioner to arrive so they could begin. He was in a relatively good mood. The success of the bazaar buoyed his hopes. Six pounds, fourteen shillings and three pence, which would perhaps translate to one hundred bricks, some planks for the doors and three-by-four iroko timber for the door frames.

'I have a lot to be thankful for,' he would say to himself. 'More than a year in these jungles and I am not yet dead. The White Man's grave, they call it, but so far not mine.' But he could never for long keep himself from fretting about when the new church would be complete. When? When? When? Would a miracle occur? Would he one day pick up an unclaimed bag of money? Who in these parts would lose such money and make that type of miracle possible? As always in the end he muttered: '*Voluntas Dei fiat!*' – partly in faith, partly out of the realization that events occurred with little regard for his wishes.

And then it was New Year's day. But this was just another day, indistinguishable here from the day before or after it. Time in this environment showed a reluctance to be divided. His watch was the only one within thirty miles. There were days because the sun rose and set, and months because the moon phased in and out. But even the days and months merged indistinguishably into one another like the consecutive revolutions of a big wheel. There were only two seasons – the wet and the dry – both of them hot and wet to a greater or lesser extent, except for a brief cold spell of the Sahara harmattan in the middle of the dry season. Time, as he had known it in Europe, had no meaning here, for it presumed that there was a beginning and an end. One year, ten years, a century, who cared? A year from what? A century from what? The sun rose and set daily, the seasons came and went at their appointed times, without making progress. The rivers continuously poured themselves into the seas. The seas never got full and the rivers never seemed to run out of water or to tire of emptying themselves out. Life here was not linear, but cyclic and repetitious. Everyone was hitched to a big horizontal circle, and going round and round.

7

Some days later, Father Higler made his regular pilgrimage to Aba.

Aba was a trading centre, a halfway house between Europe and Africa, a mockery to both. Its premier citizens were colonial administrators, the less favoured veterans of other colonial adventures reaping their rewards on this piece of empire and avenging their lot on native underlings or young men whose survivability was being tested before they could be promoted to higher things elsewhere, export-import officers of European firms, who with their frail wives spent the hot afternoons at the Catering Rest House, chafing and cursing at the heat, disparaging the natives, and swilling pools of scotch and soda.

There were also the natives, those whose smattering of education had turned into vulgar dilettantes and compulsive imitators of the insundry ephemera of Europeanism, junior grade officers and clerks, traders and middle men, artisans and idle hands. Their low houses, roofed in thatch and corrugated zinc, huddled together along narrow unpaved streets, muddy when it rained, dusty when it did not, all a respectful distance from the European Quarters, where the non-natives lived.

On this particular trip Father Higler was loaded with money from the bazaar and found himself happily able to buy cement and timber – enough to give the masons their customary half-day's work for a few weeks. He also bought things to eat and drink, medicine to keep the fevers in check and got a haircut at the Catering Rest House.

On his return from Aba, Father Higler found Philip ill at ease.

'It is not your health, Philip? What then is it?' A pause during which the priest stared hard at the servant who now stood frozen with a tray of breakfast dishes in his hands. There was a sudden clicking of a decision in the priest's face, a suspicion. 'Is it by any chance that other business of sacrifices to the jujus?'

'Yes Fada.' Philip controlled the impulse to exhale precipitately.

'But why? I thought we went over that and came to a conclusion.' He paused, reckoning his own thoughts, urging kindness and understanding on himself. 'Didn't we agree that there was nothing to do, that you should do nothing but forget the whole thing? Have you gone back now on that decision?'

'Fada there are some things . . .'

'You are a Christian now, Philip. Your faith is the most important thing you have, including your life itself. You must guard it with all your strength. You renounced the old paganism at your baptism. You don't want your baptism to have been in vain, do you?'

'No Fada.'

'Well then, banish all thoughts of those sacrifices from your mind once and for all. It is no sin to be tempted, but when we indulge a temptation beyond what is reasonable, then we risk blame for the consequences.'

'Fada it is not easy.'

'Of course it is not easy being a good Christian. It is a yoke, a cross. Our Lord said: "If a man would come after me, let him deny himself, and pick up his cross."'

'I suffer enough, Fada, I think.'

'None of us ever suffers enough, Philip.' Father Higler was surprised at Philip's insistence and uncharacteristic argumentativeness.

'I do not sleep at night.'

'What do you want from me? My permission, my endorsement of the pagan sacrifices?' A chuckle dried up in the priest's throat. 'I am surprised,

Philip. And somewhat disappointed. Such permission is not mine to give; there can be no such permission. You cannot serve God and the native jujus as well.'

'Fada, I already choose to serve God. Even though I am Njoku, the other Fada convinced me to be a Christian and I agreed. Since then I serve only God without looking back.'

'Fine. Go on serving Him. Don't look back now.'

'Do not be angry with me, Fada, but I am afraid.'

Father Higler exhaled, swallowed and then looked at Philip. 'I am not really angry with you Philip.'

'Does Fada have anything he can give me as protection?' He fingered a cluster of medals around his neck.

'I thought you said you sold those medals?'

'I bought some myself. I paid for them, Fada.'

'The greatest protection we can have is God's grace. If you are in a state of grace, Philip, you have nothing to fear, okay?'

'Yes Fada. I would like to go to confession Fada.' A smile, gratifying to Father Higler, tugged at the servant's dark features.

'Yes, of course, Philip. All God demands from each of us is faith.'

'I have believed, Fada, with all my heart.'

'Fine. But you must never let that belief falter.'

'I am sorry, Fada, but sometimes we need to hear God's voice to know that He is still there.'

'If you listen hard enough, you will hear it.'

'Yes Fada. I will listen, Fada.'

'Tell me, how's your uncle Nwala?'

'Fada he is still not well. Any day he makes now we count for him, but we count no days for him beforehand.'

'That's bad. Have you spoken to him lately? Have you spoken to him at all since the incident?'

'No Fada. He has commanded me not to come near him.'

'Tell me, why does the man dislike you so?'

'Since I join church.'

'Since you joined the church? You mean that is the sole basis of his dislike of you?'

'Yes Fada. That is what he says.'

'But why? Why is he that dead set against the church? For himself and for others?'

'Fada I am next to him in age in our compound. All those between me and him are dead. He thinks I should help him to serve the family jujus.'

'Well, Philip, you have made the wiser choice. That is all I can say. As for your uncle and the basketfuls of family jujus, we can only ask God's forgiveness on their behalf. But I must have a talk with the man.'

Philip shrugged. 'Maybe Fada can try, but it will be no good.'

'I will try,' Father Higler said.

And so a few days later Father Higler went to see Nwala. There were no adults at home when he reached the compound. The wife who was supposed to be attending the sick man had gone somewhere in the backyard to pick up some twigs for a fire. One of the older children led him into the sick room.

'*Nna-nna,*' the boy called.

'What? Who is it? Ah!'

'The Fada has come to see you.'

'Who?'

'The Fada. The White Fada who lives in the mission.' With that the boy left to rejoin his playmates.

Nwala lay on a mat on the floor of what had to pass for a sitting room – it had several stools of raffia bamboo. His face was turned towards the wall, his back dangerously close to a fire, now dead, although somebody must have been blowing it earlier because the sick man and much of the furniture were speckled with ash. The room had a strong repulsive odour, a blend of human uncleanliness and the concoctions on which Nwala must have been existing during his illness. Father Higler wiped his hand subtly across his face.

Nwala began to roll over on his back, a slow and painful process during which he cringed and grunted. He had been reduced to a tall skeleton with a thin, brown coating of skin. His face was sunken, especially around the eyes; his head was bony and its hair seemed to have stopped growing. His jaw was thrust out; his mouth hung open, giving the suggestion of a snarl, and lower down on his chest his ribs stuck out prominently as if he had been systematically starved to the very bones. He looked pitiable. Father Higler could remember him, tall and muscular and striding and impatient. To see him there now so reduced to mere bones and so helplessly patient would have evoked the sympathy of his bitterest enemy. When he finally completed the task of rolling over, his eyes opened slowly and an expression escaped from his lips. 'Ah!' It was an utterance whose import Father Higler could not decipher, whether it was an expression of disgust, surprise or anger. Could the man recognize him? 'Ah!' he said again. The way he looked at him with his eyes half-closed was frightening. There was always something in the face of the dead or the dying which tended to frighten him, something he had never got used to even though as a priest he often had to attend the dying. It was in the eyes – their vacant, unbalanced, unblinking and unfocused expression. Occasionally at night when he was alone and recalled it, a chill ran through his body.

'How are you feeling today?' he asked.

'Ah,' he said. 'You have come to see me?'

'Yes. How are you?'

'Just as you see me. That is how I am. No other how. Ah!' he gasped, obviously in pain this time. The way he moved was painful to watch. He initiated each movement slowly and then proceeded to urge himself into it. Now he lifted one hand and placed it in the concavity of his belly. He was short of breath, and when he spoke he ran out of wind in the middle of his sentences. 'When the lion is sick . . . ah! . . . the antelope comes to collect an old debt . . . Ah! You have come to see me lying low. To mock me?'

'Are you feeling better today?' Father Higler asked.

'Feeling better? Feeling? I do not know how I am feeling today. How do you feel? Who sent for you to come and see me? Your pot boiler? He will never be useful to himself . . .'

'That is an unkind thing to say.'

'It is the truth. He is the son of my own bosom brother. The same penis that planted the seed to make his father also made me. It is not in my mind to curse him . . .' Abrupt silence. Father Higler shifted on his feet. Then the sick man spoke again. 'Why have you come here today? To see me die?' He turned his eyes slowly and attempted a shallow cough, and then said: 'Pull a chair and sit down.'

Father Higler did as he was bid, and sitting down was pleased that Nwala was at least not patently hostile. But he was at a loss about what to say or do, and the uncertainty made him nervous. Nwala had meanwhile closed his eyes. Shallow breaths pumped his belly in rapid movements. Where to start talking? Philip or Baptism? 'You realize,' he said, 'that it is appointed to all men to die?' The expression was a thought which had broken the sound barrier without his full permission. It fell into the silent semi-darkness of the room like a stone thrown into a serene but dirty pond. He was sorry as soon as he heard it and wondered if Nwala had heard it, for the latter made no response. He watched the hollowed face, and for all he knew the man could have dozed off or even died. Then a smile, a frightening smile, began to break through the face to which several weeks of hoary hair growth clung like dried pin worms. It was like seeing a corpse smile, a long-dead corpse, and Father Higler was slightly unnerved. Nwala could not summon enough energy to laugh, and presently he gave up the atttempt.

'You have come to see me die,' he said. 'I am going, but you should not rejoice over me. Yours will come.'

'No no,' Father Highler replied. 'I have come to see you get well and give you baptism.'

'Bap-bap-bap-what? What is that? Is that some medicine you have brought to me? Is it poison?'

'No no. It is not medicine. Not medicine for the body, anyway. It is medicine for the soul.'

'It will make my heart well?'

'Not directly. You see, baptism will rescue you from the fires of Hell, where all evil souls burn forever.'

'Ah, why, you think I am evil?' Then came that unnerving sepulchral smile.

'No, no. Not necessarily. None of us *really* is.'

'My father, did he save his soul?'

'That I do not know. No one can say, but without baptism there can be no salvation. That is what the Scriptures say.'

'My father is then burning in this hell fire of yours? . . . Ah!'

'I do not know. That is for Almighty God alone to know.'

'Why should I save my soul? What will the water you pour on my face do for me against this big, raging fire of the other world? Will it quench it? Aah! And you say my father may be burning in it already. Who told you?'

'You see, your father died in ignorance of the true God, for which he cannot be blamed. Perhaps . . .'

'Ignorance? Of what? Aah!' He exhaled heavily and then laughed as long as his breath would hold. 'You insult my father,' he said. 'You insult him in a way you should not insult him. If I was on my two feet, I would have said something to you about that. But the lion is sick and the antelope has come to collect an old debt.' He paused, then continued. 'My father was a very strong man. And wise.' He repeated the word, 'ignorance', and opened his eyes to look at Father Higler. 'Aah!' he gasped painfully. 'He was strong and wise.'

'Do you want me to baptize you?'

'No,' Nwala said thoughtfully, and there was a pause and a stillness which seemed to go beyond the room. Even the children playing outside seemed to have paused for a moment. 'No!' he repeated. 'I do not want your baptism. Keep it and your hellfire for yourself. They are both yours, White Man.' There was an air of irrevocable finality about his words. Hitherto, his illness had seemed to have made his voice weaker, but in uttering that rejection his voice was firm and masterful as of old.

Father Higler breathed a sigh of defeat, folded his hands across his chest and leaned back on the wall behind his chair.

'Have you saved your own soul?' Nwala asked at length. 'And your pot boiler?'

He sighed. He had not saved his own soul for sure, had he? There were no reserved tickets to heaven. He would have to wait and see at the Gate. 'No,' he was forced to admit. 'Not for sure. There are no guarantees . . .'

Nwala again attempted to laugh, and the efforts of his face to produce laughter made Father Higler wince with pain.

'You are a medicine man who cannot cure his own self . . . Ah!' He paused, trying to reassert himself over some pain which was trying to get the best of him. His upper teeth came down heavily on his lower lip. 'You are a white man,' he added. 'I do not know how it is where you come from. But I am from this Land, you see, and I have served it well. I have lived and worked here, and have never left it. In my life I did not steal and I did not practice witchcraft on anyone. And I did not commit any tabu. I buried my father well as our customs say. I think I have left my children enough to bury me. I tried. That is what I can say to myself as I lie here wasted. What else can a man do?'

'But that's not enough,' Father Higler said. 'Not quite. You are forgetting that a man is made of soul and body, and that the soul is more important . . .'

'You are the judge of me?'

'No, I am not judging you.'

'Do not judge me. I am older than you, and you do not know how you will be when your day comes.'

'True, but . . .'

'Are you going back to your own country, or will you stay here now?'

'I am not sure.'

'Be careful of yourself . . . Oh, I grow tired, and my breath is short. Tell your pot boiler for me – he does not speak with me these days – tell him to watch his steps and to point them back to his own people and father, and the duties that fall on his shoulder. If you had a son would you like him to be like him? . . . You see, a man cannot run away from the Land, even if he flies like a bird. He must come down to it, and it will be there waiting.'

'Why don't you like Philip?'

'Like? A man cannot talk of liking his own as if it were a thing apart. Can a man hate his own blood? I like him is why I am saying what I am saying. When I am not here any more he will have to face the things which want to hear from him.'

'You are against his being Christian?'

'What is that?'

'Being a member of my church.'

'Oh, I see.' He seemed to think. Father Higler gave him time and waited for an answer. 'No, I am not against you or him or your church. But duty. I am against a man who is blind and will not see what is his duty . . . aaah! . . . I grow tired, White Man. Talk steals away the little breath I have. Come and see me again some day before I go. It will not be long now . . .' He closed his eyes, took a deep breath and arranged his hands carefully over his belly.

Father Higler rose to his feet. 'Keep fit,' he said. 'You are sure you don't want me to baptize you?'

He stood waiting for the answer, but it never came. Finally he turned to leave the room. At the door Nwala's voice caught him. 'Do not blame a sick man for not offering kola,' it said.

'No blame. Thank you,' he replied and walked out. In the yard he tried to ingratiate himself with the children, but they did not make up to him and waited impatiently for him to leave so they could resume their games.

Near the road he met Ugochi (God's eagle feather on someone's cap), Philip's half-wit foster daughter.

'*Ndewo*,' he said.

'*Ndewo*,' the girl replied grinning.

'*Inu otu ole?*' (How are you?)

'*Adim nma.*' (I'm fine.)

'*Ngini mere isi jegh abia katechism?*' (Why don't you come to catechism?)

'Kat–, kat– . . .' A hand over her mouth, Ugochi giggled at her inability to pronounce the word.

'You know who I am, don't you?'

'Yes.'

'Who am I?'

Still grinning. 'You are our Fada at the mission. *Nna*, he works for you.'

'That's right. Why don't I ever see you at my church?'

She began giggling again. Looked at herself critically and brushed a hand across her chest. 'Like this?'

She was naked, except for a strip of loin cloth girdled around her waist and a string of beads around her neck. A stout young woman of sixteen or seventeen, her face was coarsely cut, only half chiselled in the act of creation, her nose characteristically flat and bridgeless though not large, her lips meaty. Her uncovered chest was endowed with two large mounds of ripe and lusty flesh, crowned with circular nipples of darker hue, turgid with the juices of young womanhood.

'Come as you are,' Father Higler felt prompted to say, but he could not very well say that, and mean it. He was not concentrating on what he was saying. His eyes, he felt, lingered just a little too long on the girl's nakedness. An illicit surge of blood in his veins. He struggled to repress it but succeeded only in getting himself more disconcerted. He jerked his eyes off their target, took a step as if to walk away from his feelings, but stopped, ordering himself to be still. The girl was still grinning, a small basket of cassava roots balanced on her head.

'Look,' Father Higler finally said, 'don't you have any clothes?'

She shook her head slowly.

'We have to see about that. Yes . . .' He began walking off. 'Yes . . .'

Back at the mission he stopped at the new church and sighed at its low status. But help was on the way. A brick at a time, and then some day. The Temple of Jerusalem, the Basilica of Saint Peter – they took years to build and greater men than he with far more help than he had, had been building them. He ran his hand over the bricks, walked alongside the walls, let his mind reach upwards to a height they would attain some day, the lofty spire that one day would reach up like a prayer towards heaven, outreaching the oil bean and rubber trees, a cross at its crest, a bell in its heart. This building would be something enduring, and even long after he was gone, it would stand in defiance of the weather and the forests. He stood away from the wall, tilted his head back and with a hand over his brows looked into the empty sky to where the spire would some day be. A smile broke on his face. And then once again he moved close to the wall, put his hand gently on it. Then he hit it with his clenched fist, as if to test its durability. He was reassured.

8

By hovering at the brink too long, Nwala had spent all the drama to which one death was entitled, and so overtaxed the common anticipation that when his death finally came, it was a great anti-climax. But he did die, from vaguely diagnosed illnesses which could trace their history to the wounds he received during the fight at Paul's funeral. He was given the final cleansing; the justifications of both his life and death were chanted over his body before it was committed to the earth as befits an *oke amadi*, a man of superior standing. Several days of burial ceremonies preserved through countless generations of uninterrupted tradition were staged and correctly enacted.

For four days the *Ese* drummers whipped their wild drum tattoos.

The *Avu* dancers, renowned shakers from a distant village, sang their full-throated chants to the accompaniment of assorted drums, gongs, rattlers and turtle shells.

The new widows were formally initiated into mourning in the presence of the entire village.

Men flounced before the hired music and in song and dance recounted tales of ancient valour and heroism – theirs as well as the dead man's – brandished old trophies, tarnished as well as polished.

All four days quivered with earth-shaking discharges of musket fire, in volleys and in solitaire, for it was the custom that when a man of means died several calabashfuls of gun powder were provided and anyone who owned a dane or flint gun or could borrow one had a free supply of powder with which to make booms to his heart's content.

The climax of the ceremonies came on the third day, with the usual *Igbu Ehi Isi na Ama* – the attempt by the oldest son of the deceased to decapitate a cow. As a preamble to the great event, all other activities were temporarily suspended. The guns held their fire. The dancers stopped. The *Ese* drummers muffled their drumming. A few rams and billy goats had their heads lopped off by the younger sons of the deceased.

The favoured son then came forward brandishing a blazing machete.

Running from a distance to break-neck stops in front of the *Ese* drummers. The drumming comes to a signal stop. He whirls around and eyes the cow – its neck stretched out because ropes are pulling it in opposite directions. The drumming has resumed. The running-stopping ceremony is repeated three more times. The head cutter for the last time faces the animal. Silence. Suppressed murmurs in the surrounding crowds. Anticipation. Ejaculatory words of encouragement.

Then a sudden burst of drumming by the *Ese* people!

Kwaga na ipi!

Kwaga na ipi!

The chief drummer is jeering the young man.

Hack it on the horns!

Hack it on the horns!

You can't miss the horns!

It's got such big horns!

The drummer's taunts are traditional as are the young man's threats to hack off the drummer's head instead of the cow's. Nwala's son did not achieve the ideal valour of cutting the head off in one stroke. He went wild with his second stroke, hitting one of the horns as the drummer recommended, and wound up in need of a third and a fourth stroke before the head finally fell off.

The *Ese* people broke out in their wildest drumming yet, flogging their taut goat-hides like men possessed. The gunners fired one horrendous salvo. Then the excitement simmered and men conversed.

There once was a time, they all remembered – oh yes, once was there a time, when men were really men and cut off cows' heads so cleanly their own legs were in danger from the slashing machete. Yes, days long, long ago when men were more than men. What do we eat nowadays that our bloods have gone so thin and our sinews so limp?

Nwala, in short, was properly mourned by his rightful mourners – fittingly and without drama – except for the whispered comments and questions about one mourner who should have been there but was not.

Philip.

'Where is he?' people asked.

'Where could he be?' some sighed painfully.

'At the mission!' others answered.

Pot-boiling for the White Man.

Still pot-boiling.

And only pot-boiling.

What fortunes are there in the White Man's pots?

Misfortunes, you mean? For this compound, this whole village.

He can do no better?

He can do no worse!

This is not the first time one of us has abdicated the heritage and defected from our noble customs.

True. In my life, and I am not the oldest man here, I can remember at least three corpses that we have whipped for wasting their lives while they had it, and in death leaving nothing for their burial.

We may have to thrash his corpse some day soon – this pot boiler – ten strokes for each of his delinquencies.

With neither wife nor child he will leave nothing to bury him.

Yes, he will pay somehow for all this in life or in death.

He's dead already! Better dead than alive. Walking, talking, dead!

There will not be enough of him for all the things that want a piece of him.

And his White Man. Do you remember the White Man at the trial? Out in the rain, taking pity on us inside the shelter.

If my wife must leave me I would prefer that her next husband be at least as good as I am.

A man who must eat a toad should select one that is fat and juicy.

So, this church going for which he has left everything, what is it doing for him?

Ayi! It is a proper wonder.

To go from the shelter to the open.

From the parlour to the kitchen.

From something to nothing.

From a native son to a wayfarer in one's own village.

To run and not run far.

To jump and not jump high.

Where is the meaning of it?

It has no meaning.

His testicles must be withered.

No, he must be mad.

Or dead.

Or worse!

Philip showed his face only on the first day of the mourning, and even then ever so sparingly, walking by the edges of the crowds, afraid to traverse them or to engage the eyes that scowled at him, trailed him and asked: Why? In his hut, he shut his door and barred it as if he feared forcible intrusion. But he could not escape the noises, the gunshots that boomed and boomed again, the overheard references to his name and his abdication of duty. He could not escape the turmoil which churned in his own heart, the contradictory demands and orders of the various allegiances to which he was subject. He was a rope in a tug of war, a rag wrung from two ends, a man without choice, without voice, defenceless and undefended. Duties without rewards. It was not just. It could not be just, to be so caught between irreconcilable allegiances, each fiercely jealous, neither sufficient protection against the other – captious, quarrelsome lordships, careless about rewarding virtue and services but painfully meticulous in remembering and punishing failings.

One floundered aimlessly in a featureless desert – the signposts that seemed to guide were cruel mirages. There were no real signs, no certain directions, only the turbulent swirl of uncertainty and the guarantee that before long one would go wrong and earn punishment. Only error and punishment were certain. Fear. Fear arrested the heart and shook it to submission. Where to find refuge. Threatened by a flood, one fled to higher ground. But what did one do when the rising flood waters were about to kiss the top of the hill of one's last refuge? And the hill demanded exclusive allegiance and the waters all of one's fealty?

Despair. Throw one's hands in the air and give up. Abandon one's self to the mercy – mercy? – no – the cruelty – of the gods. Was there nothing beyond despair? It was not a satisfactory state. It never really existed in full measure. A spark of hope had to exist somewhere or one would not go on living. And it was not a passive state but a condition of dynamic, though irresolute, activity, not a solution but the recognition of insolubility. Was there no action that could cure one of the torments of despair? Suicide was out, for there were particular and general judgements, resurrections and reincarnations. Suicide was further victimizing one's self when one had been sufficiently victimized already. There had to be another way of fighting fate, confronting it and fighting it.

He opened the door, gave the mourning crowd a fleeting glance, turned quickly towards the trail that led to the compound's common latrine, past the latrine, through the bushes until he emerged at the road. Then back to the mission to cook supper for the priest master.

Watching Philip serve supper, Father Higler could not be sure of the expression on the servant's face. It was a new one, a lightening of the former, thickly-knit graveness, a slight trembling of the hands connoting fear, but also a firm bite on the lips, as if he had found a new determination.

'I am really sorry about your uncle, Philip.'

'Yes Fada.'

'Is there anything I can do?'

'Fada? . . . No Fada.'

Father Higler pursed his lips and regarded Philip carefully. 'Is something . . .' he began, but then changed his mind. 'I wish your uncle would have let me baptize him. I wish to God he had!' He shrugged his shoulders. 'That is now spilled milk, isn't it? . . . Can I have a glass of water, please.'

'Yes Fada.'

Philip brought the water, waited for a few moments, then disappeared towards his kitchen, there to wait until Father Higler was done with supper. He cleared the plates, but in an uncharacteristic break from routine, he did not return a short time later to ask the priest if there was anything else he could do for him before he retired to his own place for the night.

Bedtime. Father Higler completed his office and sat in the chapel in silent contemplation, asking God in his heart to speed up the construction of the new church and to drive more converts into it. Afterwards he stood on the veranda watching the stars before finally going to bed, with the gunshots still exploding in his ears and the sharp tattoo of the *Ese* drummers reverberating in his head. In the darkness on that first day of Nwala's mourning, he had thought about the villagers out there, countless black faces milling around in the darkness, lost souls and souls on their way to being lost. He had not saved a soul that day. Not one of them!

Before he came here he used to think of hauling them in in netfuls. But the forests held them back, the soil, their gods, and jujus, rampaging devils. He could fish only with a line here, not a net. And the line often tangled in the weeds . . . The new church. Conceived in the highest hopes, hopes so heavy they seemed to weigh down the walls and forever keep them near the ground. A smaller church might have been finished in half the time this one was taking. His parishioners could barely produce enough money in one month for a row of bricks around its perimeter.

At length sleep overtook his senses. He slept fitfully.

And some hours later his ears pricked up. He thought he had heard something, but he told himself there was nothing to fear. He listened, and then heard it again, this time distinctly, a soft clash of metal upon metal, and it seemed to come from the direction of the kitchen. His heart drummed uncontrollably now. A new volley of gunfire exploded the quiet night outside. He lay still, sighing at the raffia bed which creaked horrendously with the slightest movement he made.

Resolutely, he stood, grabbed his flashlight and went out to investigate, opened the back door quietly and threw a beam of light into the darkness towards the kitchen. A human figure moved in the kitchen. His heart ebbed, his mouth dropped with fear for he realized that he was totally defenceless.

'Who's there?' he shouted into the night, steadying himself against the door frame. His hand, and therefore the light, trembled.

A figure appeared in the door of the kitchen. He sought out the face and blinded it with the powerful beam. The face stood, big and round and flat and black, glistening with the oil of dried sweat. The brows were thick and hung heavily over the eyes. The lips were meaty and the lower one drooped under its own weight.

'Philip!'

'Yes Fada!'

'You know if . . . if I had a gun I might have shot you.' He relaxed, letting out a breath and sighing. Then he lowered the light. 'What the devil are you doing here? I thought you were gone home?'

'Yes Fada.'

'Why did you come back? Did you forget something?'

'I am sorry to disturb you Fada.' He pushed something he was chewing to the back of his mouth. His gaze was cast to the ground, something not usual with him, for even though he seemed to treat his calling the way his master treated his priestly vocation, he was not really shy. 'Fada I am here now.'

'Yes,' Father Higler replied, slightly amused at the answer. 'That seems obvious enough. Come here, Philip,' he then said in a more serious tone. 'Tell me, is something the matter? Why are you here?'

Philip advanced towards him, beads of sweat on his face, despite the cool night air, the corners of his mouth twitching. He was stout and solid like a block of hardwood; his biceps were girded with a network of veins; a cross had replaced the medals that normally sat in the middle of his broad and hairless chest. He stopped a few feet from the priest and looked up once into the latter's face and then down again at the circle of light pointed at his feet.

'Fada, I can sleep here tonight?'

For a couple of moments Father Higler did not answer, as if the request was something he had to consider carefully. Then, 'Why, sure, Philip!' he said. 'Of course you can sleep here.' He had an itch to ask what the servant was running from, but he decided that the question was inadvisable at this time. 'Let's see. I don't believe I have any spare blanket. But you're welcome to the space . . . What? . . . The question prompted his lips, nudging him like the urge to vomit. But he held it back.

'My own mat Fada,' Philip said, pointing to a straw mat rolled into a tube, and leaning against the wall of the kitchen.

'Sure. You can make yourself comfortable on any corner of the parlour you wish. Come on.'

'Fada, kitchen here all right.'

'Nonsense. Come on. Get your mat.'

Philip obeyed in his usual way, which was exactly midway between enthusiasm and lack of enthusiasm. He always seemed infinitely capable of finding the dead centre. He obeyed, it seemed, because he felt it was his duty to obey, in perfect indifference to the order, whatever it was. If he had any feelings towards the order, he never revealed them.

Father Higler suggested a corner, and at once he unfurled his mat and spread it out. The priest sat down by the dining table, and Philip at his invitation sat down on the mat. 'Why? . . .' The question once again began crawling up his throat, but he suppressed it.

'Well, good night Philip,' he finally said, almost reluctantly.

'Yes Fada,' Philip replied.

Father Higler paused, looking at him, then suddenly firming up his mind, walked into the bedroom and slammed the door harder than he intended. But his mind was still on Philip, and like a detective, was feverishly pursuing various false leads to explain the servant's behaviour. It had to be something related to Nwala's death, but the blame for what happened on that day of Paul's funeral had already been disposed of. The sacrifices! Was Philip in physical danger from his relatives? Were they plotting to kill him? Why didn't he say? . . . And in that event what sanctuary did the rectory offer him? His danger would become their danger, and both of them together were as helpless as one.

In the meantime he fell asleep.

Some time in the middle of the night he heard a deafening noise and than a human voice emptying itself like a river in flood into the darkness. Louder! As if a life depended on it, as if the boat on which a sailor had sailed to a desert island was leaving him behind and was about to drop instantaneously out of earshot and he had to get attention that very moment or be marooned forever. Then quite suddenly he recognized the voice as his own, and began wondering how it had left him and become isolated.

A few moments later, the realization washed over him. He was now fully awake and found himself standing beside the bed. He felt for the bed and sat down, puzzled. He had been having a nightmare, he figured. He tried to recall what it was about but could not. He wondered. Nightmares were usually vivid and memorable.

A rustle in the parlour made him start. It was then that he remembered Philip. That made the puzzle even knottier. He must have awakened the servant. He tried hard to remember why he had started shouting. Somehow it seemed to him that the first voice he had heard had not been his. Philip? Philip!

His heart leaped into his throat. He saw the servant with his throat slit and with a rusty dagger plunged into his heart. He shook the thought off his mind, but for some reason he could not avoid fearing the worst for Philip, and as he stealthily approached the living room door he was afraid to open it lest his worst fears be confirmed. He stood there trembling, while the door itself seemed to dissolve away and several wild phantasms danced before his eyes, all of them drenched with blood. He took another step toward the door, and was almost knocked down by the realization that it was open. His heart fluttered. But then he reasoned: If they wanted him also – whoever or whatever they were – the door certainly had not forestalled them. He thought of sneaking up to the door and then quickly or quietly bolting it, but then he wound up chiding his own cowardice. The flashlight! He tiptoed back towards the bed and fetched it. He got more than light from it – confidence and a feeling of power, as if it emitted a lethal ray which summarily annihilated whatever he beamed it at.

Philip was sitting on the mat in the nook, his back against the wall, his knees drawn up, his right hand lying beside him holding on to a rosary. A breath of relief escaped from Father Higler's open mouth. He shone the light on Philip's face to be sure, and the latter did not dodge the glare by looking down or away, but stared directly into the blinding light. 'Philip!'

'Yes Fada.'

He breathed out again in relief, went back into the bedroom and brought out the lamp, turning it up. Then he sat down and tried to collect his thoughts.

'Philip, did you hear me shouting?'

'Fada?'

'I said, did you hear me shouting a short time ago?'

'Yes Fada.'

Father Higler shook his head and smiled and tried to make light of the whole thing. 'Believe me,' he urged, 'I don't do this every night.' He tried to chuckle. What was he trying to explain anyway? He looked at Philip. 'I've never done this before. I believe I was having a nightmare. Isn't it strange that the first time I have one is when there is someone here to hear it? Did you hear anything else? Were you awake before?'

'Fada, the thing is I think I shout in my own sleep and wake you up. And then you – I am sorry, Fada.'

'Oh!' The word blew out of Father Higler's mouth. He was extremely glad, so glad he felt like embracing Philip or pumping his hand in a fit of thankfulness. 'My goodness,' he said, 'you too were having a nightmare?'

'Yes Fada. Bad dream.'

'What? . . .' Once again he checked himself. He had thought to ask what the servant's nightmare was about. He looked at him as he sat on the mat, holding on to the rosary, but at the same time trying to conceal it from the priest's attention. Then Father Higler noticed the imprint of a machete under the mat. 'What is that?' he asked.

'Fada?'

'What is that there? A machete?'

'Yes Fada.'

'Why do you carry it?'

'Fada, for protection.'

'Hmmh.' He continued to assess the servant, and as he did the old question began to crawl up his throat again. Again half his mind counselled against it. But then again with a sudden impulse which he indulged before he could argue it down he called out: 'Philip!' He would not go on tormenting himself with this unresolved quandary. 'Are you afraid of something? Are you running away from something by staying here tonight?'

'Fada?'

'Don't beat about the bush. Just tell me. Are you running from something?'

'Fada, I am awright.'

'I believe it has something to do with your uncle's death. Or are we still wrestling with those sacrifices that you were supposed to make?'

The left corner of the servant's mouth twitched ever so slightly. 'Fada,' he said, and then he faltered. The shadow which the lamp cast off him was sharp and dark and exactly his size. It coincided exactly with him and seemed to struggle with the real him for the sole possession of some desirable aspect of the meeting place of the two walls where he was wedged. 'Fada,' he said for the second time, 'nothing is going to happen to me.'

The statement belied itself.

'Yes,' Father Higler said. 'But what is it that you are safe from?'

Philip made several starts but did not answer. He extended his legs to their full length, placing one on the other, with his heels reaching just beyond the edge of the mat and his hands folded into each other and thrust like a wedge between his laps. He looked up briefly, seemingly to note the expression on Father Higler's face, and then he looked down again. He seemed to focus on his toes, twitched them. 'Fada . . .'

Father Higler's eyes widened with expectation.

'Fada . . . Fada, you know I am next oldest to Nwala.'

'Yes? . . .'

'Now that he is dead I am the oldest.'

'I see. I see . . . Well, well. Now I see everything. All the family responsibilities, including the family jujus, are now your keep, correct?'

'Yes Fada,' answered Philip exhaling.

Father Higler's voice became less anxious than it had been earlier. 'I don't see that there should be any reason for prolonged meditation on the matter, do you?' He shrugged his shoulder. 'Where is the dilemma? I don't see any cause for indecision. You're simply not available. You are now a Christian. The entire village knows that.'

'Fada? . . .'

'Someone else can service the jujus. Or better still they can dismantle them, burn them or throw them in the bush."

'Fada, I am also Njoku.'

'It seems like you want to be everything but a good Christian, Philip.'

'Fada, I try.'

'Then try harder! What is this En-en-en-this thing anyway with which you are associated?'

'Fada may not know it, but my first name, the one they gave me at my birth is Njoku. Ihi Njoku is the god of the farm. When I was born, they consecrated me to him, to serve him.'

'That is all rubbish. And I am sorry to say that at this time of night my patience is thin. But tell me, is anyone else in the village burdened with so many obligations as you? In any case you know my answer. I have had reason, sadly, to give it to you many times recently. I realize that your uncle is dead and I sympathize. But apart from your own faith which seems in danger enough, you have to think of not giving the scandal to other members of our church. Why, Philip? Why don't you, instead hedging towards this grave mortal sin, why don't you see that there is nothing – nothing – in the jujus? You can make one for yourself any time. The only power they have is in the superstitions in men's hearts. That's all.'

'But Fada, their power is like this cross which I am wearing. It does not come from what it is made of, but what it is.'

'What you believe it is. How could you compare the Holy Cross to those jujus! It is important to realize, Philip, that some beliefs are superior to others. Where is the faith you received? What have you done with it? How in the world can you compare the Cross to those infernal contraptions . . . Oh, all right, Philip, it's the middle of the night. Sleep soundly. In the morning after mass you can go to your relatives and tell them "*Non* . . ."' A big yawn caught him in the middle of the statement. ' "*Non serveam*," ' he concluded when the yawn had run its course. ' "I will not serve." That's what you will tell them, okay? And that will be that! . . . Good night.'

He took the lamp off its hook and returned to the bedroom, leaving the servant in darkness. Shut the door between them quietly, casually, as if he really did not mean to do it. Then he noiselessly slipped the bolt home, crawled into bed, blew out the light and pulled the mouth of the mosquito netting close. He tried to think, but sleep quickly arrested his senses and made off with him, not gently, but roughly, like a band of angry natives carrying him down a steep, rocky, bumpy road, into a dark, dark valley.

9

Days passed. Mass. Catechism. Choir practice. Forays into the market and other village gatherings for converts. Wishful, prayful perambulations around the new church.

Ash Wednesday. The parishioners came forward and knelt before the altar and Father Higler rubbed blessed ashes on their faces to remind them that one day they would all be dead, buried and rotten in their graves – their curse for being the lost sons of Adam, who, countless years before, had sinned on their behalf and had frittered away a blessed inheritance that might have been theirs. But still there was hope. If they behaved themselves, they would share in Christ's blessed resurrection. For –

"Those who are afflicted by the certainty of dying may be consoled by the promise of future immortality."

Lent also meant Stations of the Cross on Fridays.

'We adore thee, O Christ, and we bless thee – Because with thy Holy Cross thou hast redeemed the world!'

A plenary indulgence was attached to each successful completion, with the usual stipulations.

Late March. By now plenty of bush had been cut down around the village in preparation for the new farming season and lay waiting for the fires that would baptize them into readiness for planting. The harmattan had gone, the heat had returned and poured down from the sky with few clouds to hinder it. But as time went on, the normal reply to a greeting of 'Have you seen such heat?' became 'It cannot be many days now.' Old men would shade their brows with one hand, frown towards a favourite horizon and declare: 'Yes, I see it clearly. What the sky has held, it will soon let the earth have.'

This year as always, the first storm of the season, was an unholy hybrid of Pentecost Sunday and Lucifer's rebellion. Lightning rattled and thunder boomed. Branches snapped before the howling winds, and whole trees were uprooted in an impressive display of brutal forces, as always intimidating to Father Higler because of the uncertainty of his inner and outer defences. The rain drummed for about an hour, and then it was over, as if on a signal. The air was cleansed, discharged, fresh again. Life awakened once more in the village.

'Fada?'

'Philip!'

'Is Fada all right?'

'Yes, I am fine. How about you? I was looking for you. You didn't tell me you were leaving.'

'Fada I run to my house and see what I can do against the rain which was coming. The rain catch me before I am able to come back.'

'Your wood is thoroughly wet. The roof of the woodshed is gone!'

'Oh God! . . . I want to come back in front of the rain, before the wind start to blow too hard, but it started to rain all of so sudden.'

'Tell you what, Philip? I think the storm blew away everything you served me for lunch. So, how about night chop for me quick-quick, okay?'

'Yes Fada.' Philip beamed. He was always enthralled whenever the priest-master extended to him the gratuity of a friendly tease. It was the rare, unexpected gift, something unnameable – a token of appreciation, acknowledgement of service, the plucking of a common chord of humanity which made both of them commonly subject to laughter and sorrow, to pain and pleasure, even though they were separated by age, race and position.

Later, at supper, Father Higler invited Philip to eat with him. Surprised, even a little embarrassed, Philip declined.

'I know you have not eaten supper,' Father Higler said, forestalling the excuse Philip was about to use. 'So don't bother to tell me that you have.'

'Fada, it is not that I have eaten; it is because I am not hungry.'

'But you must be hungry. You have not eaten since lunch.'

'Fada, that lunch is still sitting in my belly. Too, when I work in the kitchen I bite things here and there. That also makes me full.'

'Aha! No wonder you have almost been starving me to death recently. After all the biting you do, there isn't much left for me.' He laughed.

'Not so Fada.'

'You can have tea with me anyway.'

Philip stood silent for a while. No excuse offered itself quickly enough, and in the meantime Father Higler said: 'Go and get it started. Don't bother to think of any more excuses.'

Philip went as he was sent and returned with the tea kettle not long afterwards.

'Tough meat this!' Father Higler said, switching the bulge on his cheek from one side to the other.

'Fada's teeth not strong?' Philip ventured.

'Teeth! These are not even teeth.'

Philip grinned.

'What are you laughing at?'

'Nothing, Fada.'

They both fell silent while Father Higler continued to eat. The storm dragged down darkness earlier than usual.

'Philip?' the priest said after a while.

'Yes Fada.'

'Are you afraid?'

'Of what, Fada?'

'The jujus. The sacrifices you were supposed to make and didn't make, taking over the family jujus – you didn't do that, did you?'

'No Fada.'

'And nobody is harassing you about any of that, are they now?'

'No Fada.'

'Another person has become juju priest in your place?'

'Yes Fada.'

'Well then. In that case you've done well, and I'm very glad. You shouldn't have any more worries . . . But tell me, how did you finally resolve to do the right thing? The last time I talked to you, I didn't seem to get very far.'

Philip shrugged his shoulders and then exhaled. 'Fada, I do not know what to say. In life a man makes decisions and makes choices. We have a saying that when fate leaves a big calabash of bad wine in front of your door, usually you have to drink it all by yourself. After I talked to you I spent a long time in thought, and then I did what I thought I could.'

'Ha-ha. So you drank your bad wine all by yourself, huh? Well, I'm glad, Philip. I'm very glad.'

The priest wanted to converse further, but it was impossible to draw Philip out. Most of the time the communication between them was made up of questions and answers, instructions and obedience. Father Higler made inquiries, and Philip supplied terse answers. Something was still amiss in Philip's life. He had become as familiar with the servant's face as he was with the pages of the mass book which he read daily. He had learned to differentiate its shades and its lines, the way a master critic notes the subtle strokes of a genuine master. And he could read a silent storm raging underneath the seemingly placid face. No, something nipped at Philip's heart. His mood seemed to deepen, his eyes to fall lower as evening approached. It was as if he did not want to go home, but was afraid to ask his permission to stay at the mission. In fact, he suspected that on more than one occasion recently Philip had quietly slept in the kitchen.

Philip stood up.

'Where are you going?'

'To the kitchen, Fada, to get the other lamp. The globe is dirty and I want to wash it.'

When Philip returned with both lamps, he was for some reason grinning, much to Father Higler's surprise. Laughter was not a frequent indulgence for the servant.

'What the devil are you laughing at?'

Philip burst out laughing aloud.

'Goodness me, Philip! You can even laugh. Ha-ha-ha . . .

Overtaken by laughter himself, Father Higler slouched over his plate until his beard was in his stew. 'Oh my goodness! Get me a rag. You have to tell me what it is, Philip, that you are laughing at.'

'Nothing, Fada.'

'Come on. Don't lie. You just don't go around laughing like this every day.'

'Fada, it is really nothing. Only a little thing that happened when I was a little boy. I do not know how it manage to come into my mind now-now. I think it is because I take the light away and leave you in darkness.'

He pressed Philip until he heard the entire story. It made him laugh then, and again and again when on occasion he would recall it. In bed that night, for instance, he thought about it and grinned into the darkness. The story had given a new dimension to the lacklustre servant, a human dimension. Philip was at one time a happy and prankful youngster, not always the sombre and morose adult that he now was. Had there been a natural development from that gay childhood to the adulthood? Where was the hitch, the turning point? Was it his mother's death when he was nine years old that had choked the mirth out of his life and turned him into a hard, emotionless man?

The story in itself was not exceptional. But it was this simplicity and ordinariness that gave it its impact. 'When I was a little boy, Fada, and we eat evening chop late at night because my mother did not come back early from market. There were two other children who stayed with us whose mother was my mother's sister . . .' He could not continue the story for laughing. 'Fada, if while we were eating, the water was gone from the *otukpo* my mother says, "You, you just drank the last of the water, go and get more from water pot outside. Take the light so that you do not fall over anything." Fada, we all ate from the same pot and the pieces of meat and fish in the soup we pushed to one side of the pot so that my mother would share them among everybody when we all finished . . . ' He broke into another laugh. 'The little pieces of fish were many. See? Nobody counted them. Nobody knew how many pieces altogether. So now with the light gone somebody can put his hand in the pot and carry away a piece of fish and chew it quickly before the light come back . . .'

'I see,' he said. 'So you were all little thieves, eh?'

'The thing is that my mother know what we do. She count the little pieces of fish with her eyes. Then when the light was gone she pull away the pot, so that if you try to thief a piece of fish you stick your hand on the bare ground instead of the pot because the pot is not there any-more . . .'

'Aha. Very clever . . . Very clever!'

'Sometimes my mother pull the pot away and then set her own hand as a trap for you, so that when your hand come around searching for the pot in the darkness, she catch it and say: "Whose hand? . . . Thief!" We children begin to play the same trick too. As soon as the light was gone we start waving our hands in the darkness and catching one another and shouting "Thief!" We began to catch my mother's hand too as she tried to lay it in wait for ours . . .'

'Did you like your mother, Philip?'

'Yes, Fada.'

'What did she look like? Describe her for me.'

'She a nice woman.'

'What do you mean? What do you remember most about her?'

'Fada,' Philip began, 'I do not remember well.' His eyes narrowed. 'She just nice.' Sadness came into his voice and into his eyes. He no longer spoke with the exuberance and excitement with which he had started the story.

Father Higler regarded him steadily. He would have liked to hear more of the stories of his childhood, but it would have been heartless to press him to tell more of them at this time.

'Very funny,' the priest said in a tone that sounded false. 'So, that's what you did in the dark, eh?'

Philip grinned. This was his adult grin, not the radiant, unrestrained grin that had lit his face a few moments earlier. It was just a mere parting of the lips, an act he performed consciously as a polite social token rather than an uncontrolled submission to mirth.

Father Higler pushed the plates away, drew a large mouthful of water and proceeded to swallow it slowly. Then suddenly he looked up at Philip and asked: 'When are you ever going to get married, Philip?'

The question rocked Philip to his very foundations. His eyes fluttered; he raised his hand, opened his mouth, futilely, tried to control himself, shrugged, cleared his throat, vainly sought an expression. At length he regained control of himself, and staring fixedly in front of him said:

'Fada, I have married before!'

'What? You, Philip, have been married before?' It was now the priest's turn to be flustered, to search in vain for the succinct expression of his surprise. 'Fantastic! Why did you never tell me?'

Philip shrugged. 'Chance never come Fada when I could tell you.'

'Well, well, well,' Father Higler exhaled. 'What happened to your wife?'

'She died.'

'Oh! . . .'

Silence, then a sigh. 'I'm very sorry, Philip. Very sorry.' He watched the servant's face for the expressions that emerged and dissolved thereon. 'This happened a long time ago?'

'It was making one year she died, when the other Fada come.'

'Father Schlotz?'

'Yes Fada.'

'I'm really sorry, Philip . . . My, it's been quite an evening, with the horrendous storm and these sad tales, first your mother and now this about your wife . . . And you never wanted to marry again?'

'No Fada.'

'Why not? A wife might cheer you up, help you carry your daily burdens.'

Philip held his breath for several moments, then released it heavily. 'It is difficult to say, Fada, why I never marry again.'

'How did your wife die? A fever of some kind?' He should not have asked, and he realized his mistake as soon as the words had left his lips. 'I am sorry, Philip. You don't have to answer.'

'I answer Fada, and get it out. She died in having a baby. That is how she died.'

'Merciful God!'

The words dropped out of the priest's mouth without his consciously willing them. No manner of death – as if there was a choice of manners – was preferable, but there seemed to him something cruel and painful in a mother's dying in childbirth. His mind flitted off on a wayward course, on a series of wayward courses defining no pattern. He sighed and sighed again at the seemingly unequal distribution of burdens and favours. Where was almighty God in all of this? Were abstractions like fate merely subterfuges for the divine alter-ego erected by the timid human spirit in order to keep from assailing God directly with the inconsistencies rampant in his administration of the universe? Faith notwithstanding, one had to admit – on the compulsion of honesty, insist – that on the basis of what we could perceive with the faculties given us – and those were all we had – the ways of God were truly incomprehensible. Illogical, according to our human logic, which, after all, was the only logic we knew.

'I'm sorry, Philip,' he said again. 'Terribly sorry.'

From that day on, Father Higler was overwhelmed by a surge of human

sentiment for the servant, sentiment that defied faith and paid little attention to theology. His heart went out in understanding, an empathy which
he had never quite managed before. He could see a pattern in the events
of Philip's life. There had been, he was sure, other sacrifices during the
wife's difficult labour, incantations of justification, prayers and libations
to the whole wretched league of jujus and idols. All to no avail. And then
less than a year later, Father Schlotz had appeared on the scene and given
the promise of a new day, a more powerful, universal, eternal, provident
and understanding God. And Philip had been one of the first to enlist in
order to find refuge. 'What refuge, Oh God, is there for him here!'

The local seers were infinitely resourceful in discovering curses which
one carried through various reincarnations, and no doubt they would have
ascribed the poor woman's difficulties in labour to some kind of curse on
her or on Philip. Then the so-called defection from his duties to the *Ihi
Njoku*. The sacrifices he was supposed to make because of the blood that
was spilled at Paul's funeral. His refusal to become a juju priest in place of
Nwala and a chaplain to his younger relatives. These – all of these and
perhaps more – against an uncertain salvation.

In his little chapel, after Philip had gone, Father Higler lifted his eyes
to the sanctuary lamp, the island of light surrounded by a sea of darkness,
sending a trail of smoke toward the raffia latticework of the chapel roof.
The quivering flame caught the altar and its dressings in shaky shadows,
the vases of bougainvillea and Pride of Barbados like silhouettes of ancient
cathedrals and the crucifix behind the tabernacle as a solitary spectator to
the life and death play of a moth and a wall gecko.

Sitting down, he exhorted his mind towards God and faith and away
from the imponderable mysteries that had to wait for the Beatific Vision
for their elucidation. But at length prayers stopped issuing from his lips
and he sat silently regarding the altar, bathing in the silence, drinking the
solitude – a sort of situation, he fancied, in which one holy enough and
favoured enough might see a vision of an angel or the Blessed Virgin.
What was his claim to such loftiness? Was coming to Africa by itself
enough, a sort of plenary indulgence such as was awarded to people who
went on the Crusades? Had coming to Africa improved his chances of
eternal salvation, wiped away his past life? One became liable at the age of
reason. No, one was liable from birth because of Original Sin. One was
just liable.

His father. His brother. His mother with her glasses perched on her
nose, her blue apron, her hair rolled into a knob at the back of her head.
Clare. He hesitated at the thought of Clare, but the mood urged him on.

Where was she now? Her hair was probably grey like his, and the rings had started to form around her eyes and neck. But these features he imagined on her were artificial, for the Clare he remembered was only a little over twenty-five, with sky-blue eyes and straw-blonde hair which was always getting into her eyes. What might she have heard about him? Could she have learned of his desertion from the Army? They would have been together now, he and Clare. And happy? And content? Was there any contentment on this side of Beatific Vision? And wasn't he happy now? Of course he was. The yoke he wore was a sweet yoke – was it? He had chosen it voluntarily – had he?

His battalion had been sent on a suicide mission to distract and draw the onslaught of a flank of the German divisions which were pouring in through Belgium. The firing had begun before they could finish digging their trenches. Officers barking orders. Wounded men groaning. The boom of shells. Muffled whine of deadly bullets. His friend, Le Roux. They had exchanged foxholes – he the smaller man had dug the deeper one. Exchanged graves, for Le Roux had been hit shortly afterwards and killed. How close death sometimes came to the living, sniffed at them, then went on his way . . . The promise to become a priest if he should ever get out alive. Would he have made the choice, the covenant, a second time? Actually he had done better when he decided to leave the monastic life for a higher form of service here.

A tear fell – pat – on his breviary, and startled him. He wiped it off, and sighing, emerged from his brooding. Rose. Commended his heart, sleep, and faith to God, genuflected and walked out. Pulled the chapel door shut and padlocked it. Stood on the veranda and stared into the infinitely unfathomable and featureless darkness, listened to the discordant chorus of frogs and toads and wondered what else was out there that he could neither see nor hear.

Back in his bedroom, he put out the light and slipped into bed, shut his eyes and began fingering his rosary beads.

Philip. Poor Philip. Me. Help us, O God. Thy faith is the evidence of things which appear not. We believe not because we see, but we see because we believe.

10

'White Man!' a voice said behind him.

Startled, he turned around to confront a shrivelled human form standing in the dusk like a sinister apparition, some miscarried evolution of the jungle, a bald dome with a tiny plug of hair at the fontanelle, a thin beard like that of an oriental patriach.

'Good evening,' Father Higler said, trying to be cheerful. 'How is your health?'

'I manage to sustain both my life and my aches.'

'We all do. We have to.'

They shook hands – arthritic, bony fingers with swollen joints, a grip consciously firm. The face was a piece of corrugated brown leather loosely pasted on the skull. The lips, partially lost behind the beard quivered continuously like a rabbit's, as if their owner was constantly repeating something to himself which no one else could hear. He had a steady serpentine gaze originating from deep in his skull where his eyes had receded, filtered through folds of skin and long, grey lashes. This was Ahamba, the man behind the voice, owner of the inimitable chuckle, old, gaunt and physically wasted, and bare, except for his *ogodo*, a strip of cloth passed between his legs and held in place with a raffia belt.

'You look at your church?'

'Yes.'

'Big. Very big. What you do with it so big? . . . When you finish it?'

Father Higler pulled his lips together and exhaled heavily, driven as always to the brink of despair whenever he thought of the distantly deferred date when this church would be complete. 'I don't know,' he replied. 'Next year. Two years, three, ten! Maybe never! I cannot tell you.'

'A long time.'

'Yes, a very long time.'

And he was sucked at once into the inescapable mire of self blame. If he had not wanted such a big church! But he wanted – needed – a church which was worthy of God and the task that had to be done here, a church that would impress itself on the large skies and the endless forests, as well as the pagan villagers, a church capable of standing up to the heaviest onslaught that could be mounted by man or spirit or untamed nature. Better no church at all than a humble building!

'But I find it strange, White Man, it is strange that you come here to build a big church like this, bigger than the people in it. You have not so many. Why did you come here to build it?'

Father Higler struck his fist affectionately at the brick wall. 'This, my friend, is a church of hope. I have come here to spread the Word, to set a light on a high stand, on a hill top, so that it may illumine the hearts of men all around. Men of this village and of other villages all around. I came to bring both the Light and the Hope here.'

'I have looked into your eyes,' Ahamba said, 'and did not find them to be brimming with hope. But your church is yours. Tell me, though, were you sent here or did you come on your own?'

'I was sent.'

'Who sender?'

'God.'

'A god. He talked to you in a dream? You heard his voice?'

'Yes.'

'Ah, but still, my friend, your god, like you, is a wayfarer among us. You both came to us, not we to you. We are not a jealous people, but hospitable like our gods. "Build your place, and we are sure there are people in this village who will give your god a trial worship." That was what we told the one who came before you. There is room in this land and in the hearts of many of our people for a guest and refugee god. *Egbe bere ugo bere* – you have heard the saying.'

'You don't understand,' Father Higler retorted, weighing his breviary between his palms. 'You don't understand at all. I am not here to add one more name to your bursting league of gods. The God I have brought – brought is your word not mine – the God I have come to reveal to you, is the only one and only true and eternal God. Creator of the universe. All knowing and all powerful. Refugee God? How can a king be a refugee in his own kingdom. This is the one God there is, my friend.' He thrust a solitary finger into the evening sky. 'One!'

'And you say he is not new.'

'He who exists outside time and beyond space cannot be new. Our knowledge of him may be called new because he has chosen to reveal himself slowly.'

'But we do not know him here.'

'That's right. Most of you do not know him yet. And that is part of the reason for this building. To bring him to you, togther with the *new* message of this salvation for all men.'

'Nothing is new, my friend,' Ahamba said, placing a foot on a broken brick and his chin on the rounded end of the tall staff he carried. 'Newness is but a blink in time's roving eye. Everything passes without fail into the past, into age, even before the word is spoken. And what salvation can you bring us who were never lost . . . Akhee-khee-khee! I am forced to laugh, White Man, because you think we are lost, and it is you, the wanderer among us, who must save us. Akhee-khee-khee! Look about you. See the coming darkness? . . .'

Father Higler lifted his eyes to the thickening dusk, the afterglow of the sunset waning away in the west like fading rose petals and drying blood stains, and to his rectory and Philip's kitchen from where supper smoke was rising reluctantly, as if an angry god had rejected the servant's evening sacrifice. He then faked a smile at the old man.

'Are we swallowing this darkness, as we stand here now, or is it swallowing us? Does the drowning man swallow the pond in which he drowns? . . . You will save us. And you expect us to agree, merely because you have told us to? A messenger brings token of his ambassadorship. You have talked about wonders, and miracles impressive to the eye, but you have shown us none. Yet you expect all of us to abandon ourselves to your care and tutelage. Akhee-khee-khee! We may yet be lost, my friend – your people and the D. O. are turning our ways bottom-up. But at this moment in time's seamless passage, with what I can see about you, you and your followers need more salvation than the rest of us.'

'You are totally mistaken. The salvation I speak of is not an earthly thing. Nor is it a tribal thing. All people need it.'

'All White people?'

'All people. Everyone sinned in Adam and was redeemed in Christ.'

'Ah, is that not the god-man who was hanged by his own people? The happy sufferer?'

'Christ, both God and man, was crucified, yes, by his own people. Evil men, as there are evil men everywhere. In every generation.'

'So there are. But his own people would not believe his message and you ask us to?'

'In their wretchedness, the rulers of his time misunderstood and rejected his message. But others accepted it eventually, and it spread. It has been spreading ever since from the hearts and mouths of men.'

'When there are valuable rewards to reap, do men go about foisting them on others? Or do they keep them for themselves. What is your reward as evangelist?'

'These are joyous tidings. The blessings are inexhaustible. More than enough for everyone. And the new spirit is against human selfishness. It enjoins every man to share, to spread the good tiding even further, so that the Word may spread even faster and wider, until all humanity has embraced it.'

'And where were we – I have asked you before – while all this was going on?'

'And I have told you it does not matter where you were then. What matters is now. Now is the hour of salvation.'

'What matters to a tree is its leaves and flowers and not its roots? . . . As for salvation, my friend, as always I have said to you – save those who have come to you as an example to the rest of us. They are lost enough! Save him there, standing now at your doorway. He is in need of much saving.' He pointed into the deepening shadows towards the rectory, and following his waggling finger, Father Higler saw Philip silhouetted against the door of the rectory.

'*Odi ndu onwu ka nma!*' Ahamba said. 'Better dead than alive.'

'Philip?'

'That is what I hear you call him. But not the name his father gave him. He boils pots for you.'

'He took a new name at his baptism to signify his new state. In baptism a man is born again, called to a new life in God. Born of the spirit, that is, not of the flesh.'

'His spirit died long ago.'

'It will be my pleasure, Ahamba, some day to baptize you.'

'You will first see a pile of shit setting off fiery sparks before you get to baptize me.'

'What has Philip done? Refused to join the rest of you in the futile worship of the jujus?'

'Ah, he has told you.'

'Yes. And I am surprised that a man of your intelligence would waste his time with those things you yourselves or your fathers constructed from wood, stone, sticks, raffia weavings, animal skulls and clay you dug from a pit.'

'How much clay will you yield, White Man, at your death? Is not clay all there is to all of us?'

'No. More than that. Far more than that, for we have each a soul made in the likeness of God.'

'Which God?'

'The one true God.'

'Mmmmh. Are not all gods true to themselves and to their divinity, if not to us? But the reason I have approached you this evening is your pot boiler. Send him home to his duties because his pot is boiling over. You know his delinquencies.'

'Delinquencies to your idle jujus. His wife died in childbirth after, I'm sure, you all helped him to offer innumerable sacrifices and incantations of justification. He saw through the folly of the jujus and made a wiser choice.'

'Wife-death is a sad thing, but wives are always dying. He could have married another wife. And another.'

'I know Philip is not a coward, and would have been able to meet the demands of the cult, if he wanted.'

'He is something he should not be, in addition to being a coward. He ran away from initiation! Three nights he was to stay in the bush by himself. That is custom. But he ran the first night, which is something that has happened before. Many men have not the heart to face what happens in these bushes you see all around in the middle of the night. Even in the middle of the day. But to run and not come back! He ran and stayed with the other one who came before you and so become pot boiler instead of Njoku . . .'

Though deeply surprised, Father Higler nevertheless felt obliged to give an answer. 'I am sure, I feel quite sure,' he said, 'that it was not cowardice that made Philip run away, if indeed he did run away as you say.'

'Something made him. I hope ﹐ou can protect him now, as well as yourself.'

'We are safe. If it is only the jujus we have to fear.'

'You need safety. But you do not even know what you are safe from; that is the point. Sometimes we parry and dodge fake blows. The real ones then hit us . . . Akhee-khee-khee! I go now. We have a saying that if you are giving medicine to a very sick man and his prick keeps getting up, it is best to leave him alone, as he has already found a woman on the other side. Send your pot boiler home to his duties. Gird your own self with caution. Deafness can be fatal . . .'

11

Empathy. Fellow-feeling and comradeship. Father Higler now felt drawn even closer to Philip. For here in the middle of darkest Africa was a man whose life coincided with his own in the present, and in the future through their association as servant and master, and whose past also was a replica of his. Philip was no longer a faithful servant, but a brother. They were survivors of similar past hazards, co-expectants of similar futures. This meant that he was no longer alone; his life was no longer a solitary orphanage; he had found his twin, his dark reflection. For in the secret heart of the taciturn servant was trapped an echo of his own life – cowardice, desertion under fire, abandonment of love.

But Philip was reluctant to share and kept his agonies tightly clasped to his chest. Father Higler watched him come and go, probed for weak points in his impenetrable shell of reticence. But all he could get out of Philip was the usual 'Yes Fada.' He invited him to share his meals; he detained him with questions and clumsy jokes after he served the meals or cleared the table, but Philip always managed to say nothing. There were no appeals from him now, no questions like 'What do I do Fada?'

In the meantime, at the church, at the eight-day market, in fact everywhere in the village, fingers continued to point at the servant as a man doomed to some imminent catastrophe, some exemplary punishment. He had broken the scale with his misdeeds. The hooks were already in him, and for that matter in all of the church-goers – all who had dared to escape their old curses and seek new blessings in a non-native god. Was escape forbidden? The church-goers looked to Philip as the bellwether of their fortunes, for among them he had escaped the most, defected the farthest. The more cautious among them had added the new God without totally discarding the old ones, and carefully balanced their allegiances according to need. They called their wavering giving to Caesar and the new God what was due to each. Philip, on the other hand, had made a clean break, and cast his entire lot with the new God, and thus had the most to gain or the most to lose.

Father Higler was in his garden as the sun dipped behind the trees. With the recent rains the ground had exploded with a new growth of weeds, which dwarfed his young balsams and marigolds. He pulled the weeds off with more than a gardener's zeal, for he saw them not just as vagrant plant growth but as agents of the evil land bent on making his life difficult and his labours fruitless. He pulled them energetically and shook the nourishing earth from their exposed roots, and then flung them as far as he could into the bush.

'Philip,' he called.

'Yes Fada,' came the answer.

Philip stood patiently beside him where he squatted, patting the dark soil around the young shoots. He did not look up to acknowledge the servant's presence, but continued firming the earth around the young balsam, kneading the sod with his fingertips and then pressing it with the top of his clenched fists.'

'Philip,' he called again. 'Tell me, Philip, why did you join the church?'

'Fada!'

Father Higler had expected a physical reaction but nothing like what he was now witnessing – the wild stare, shaking fingers, goose pimples, switching body weight from one foot to the other.

'Fada, I join,' Philip said, munching at the words, 'I just join.' A shrug.

'That's all right, Philip. I was just asking – for my own benefit.' He tossed his head and sighed. 'I know the answer already, anyway. But that's the way almighty God works . . .' He paused with the realization that his words were meant more for himself than for the servant. But nevertheless he was impelled to continue. 'That's true. Take Saint Paul. God one day had to knock him down, off his horse, to convert him . . .' He paused again, looking at Philip's doleful face.

'You remember old Ahamba some days ago? . . .' He raised his eyebrows.

Philip bit his lips, as if he dared not let them go.

'He told me about the night you were supposed to start the ceremonies to become Njoku!'

'Oh! . . .' It was the loudest overt emotion the servant had ever allowed to escape from him. It startled Father Higler with its vehemence, and he stood, his mouth and beard dropping as the evening breezes picked up the monosyllable and fled with it into the bushes. There were tears in Philip's eyes.

'I am sorry,' Father Higler said. 'I just wanted to tell you that I am very much like you, that I too . . .'

105

But he did not finish, for before he could a fit had seized Philip. He behaved like a bottle of fizzy drink opened suddenly after prolonged agitation. He ran hunched towards a nearby palm tree, gripped it with both hands and vomited against it. Father Higler ran up to him, put his hand on his back and stood helplessly watching as the emetic urge fomented the servant's belly and nudged him violently again and again. At last he seemed to be done. Father Higler offered him a handkerchief, but he shook his head and waved it aside, stepped instead to the boundary between the priest's garden and the untamed land, plucked leaves off a branch and wiped his face and mouth.

Stooping, he poured some of the garden earth over his vomit.

'Sorry Fada.'

'Think nothing of it, Philip. It's quite all right. Do you feel better?'

'Yes Fada.'

'I believe I have some chlorodyne. Something wrong with your belly?'

'Fada, I go now?'

'Yes, Philip. Of course. But wouldn't you have the medicine first?'

'I am awright, Fada. Thank you Fada.'

He marched away into the evening, walking briskly, as if something had a hand behind his neck and was urging him forward. He lacked his usual firm-footedness.

Father Higler, hands firmed against his hips, stood watching him until he reached the edge of the mission and disappeared around the bend.

That night the moon rose early, gliding through thin layers of opal clouds higher into the azure sky, half-lighting the mysteries of the night and haunting them with peace and nostalgia. Peace. *Udo. Ndokwa.* Well-being. Peace lost, won and lost again. Unsatiated cravings. Times in other lives, other worlds, other millenia, when peace and quiet reigned and the calm was not breached, and all was bright and youthful.

Preparing for bed, Father Higler heard the swelling songs of the village youth in *oro,* the traditional moonlight carol of song and dance. Care-free youth. Ever-hopeful youth. He heard them approaching and raised his head from the pillow to fix their direction, and then listened intently to make out the words of their songs. At first he thought they were singing about death – *onwu* – but as they came even nearer, he discovered they were saluting the moon – *onwa.*

Moon! Oh Moon!
Moon!
Shining so bright
Night has turned into noonday.

They entered the mission and took a stand in front of the rectory with their drums and gongs, musical pots and turtle shells and began a brief medley of songs. They stopped and broke into a conversation when he did not emerge.

He is asleep.

He cannot be.

Even a deaf man could not sleep through this.

Perhaps we should go.

We have come, we cannot just go away.

Wait, wait. I think I hear something.

There is a light.

He is coming out.

Up the music!

There was a new burst of music as he came out lamp in hand. The singing and the drumming swelled and those who felt like it began dancing. There was no orchestration and minimal direction, just the free expression of ebullient and exuberant spirits of the young.

'Turn the light down! Turn the light down!' a few of the boys shouted at him over the din. 'We have enough light from the sky.'

He obliged, left the lamp on the veranda and stepped into their midst, under the cold light of the moon. It was no special occasion, they told him, when he inquired. They were young and happy, and it did not seem right that such bright moonlight should be wasted. So they were using it, serenading it, carrying their happiness and their joyous singing from compound to compound. And they had come to his, even if he was a stranger, to cheer his heart and invite him to join their joys. Would he join them? Were they disturbing him? He was free to go back to sleep, and they would carry their joys elsewhere and bear no grudges. No, no, he said. They were welcome. And they could stay as long as they desired, for he enjoyed their songs and their spirits.

So they made a long stand before the rectory, interspersing singing and dancing with riddles and folk tales – tales of valour and betrayal, morals and trickery. He joined them in the chorus chants and the hand clapping and tried a few dance steps to their great delight and amusement. It was a delightful night, a short sojourn into peace and forgetfulness, and when at length they left and he returned to bed he did not have time for even a single thought before sleep – peaceful, dreamless sleep, spread over him like a warm cosy blanket.

Philip did not appear the following morning, and his absence was like an irregularity in nature, akin to the absence of the sun from the sky on a clear summer morning. Father Higler said mass hurriedly; only occasionally did the spirit of the prayers he recited intrude into his preoccupation with Philip. No other worshippers were at mass that morning, and he had to serve himself with water and wine in the holy rituals, and when he turned to say 'Oremus' or 'Dominus Vobiscum' there was nobody there to hear it, except the empty gravelike pews, the brown mud walls, the poster portraits of Christ's agonies, the morning dew and the grass as well as the forests visible through the open door of the church.

At the end of mass, he divested himself and walked directly to where Philip lived.

Philip made a gallant effort when he saw Father Higler and raised himself up to a sitting position, pulling up his knees and leaning his back against the wall. But a chill seized him and shook him violently from one end to the other. His teeth chattered and his eyes danced wildly. 'I am sorry Fada,' he tried to say, as he lowered his head into his knees, but his words were chewed almost beyond recognition.

'That's all right, Philip,' he said, looking around the windowless room for a place to sit down.

'S-o-r-r-y F-a-d-a,' Philip tried to say again, just a moment before he keeled over. He lay flat on his belly, tucking his neck into his shoulders and shrinking into himself, his face buried in the straw mat.

Father Higler touched his burning chin and called him:

'Philip!'

'Fada,' he gasped in a low drowning and fitful tone.

'I will go to the mission and bring you some quinine, all right?'

'Yes Fada.'

'I'll be right back. Cheer up, old boy.'

Philip did not answer.

The priest stopped briefly at the door, looking back at the servant's prostrate form, then walked off with leaden steps, reminding himself a short time later to hurry up.

He returned with a tablespoon and a bottle each of quinine and chlorodyne, and administered to Philip a large potion of each. Philip took the spoon from him with unsteady hands, and without seeming to open his eyes, gulped down the medicines with his countenance a perfect neutral. He made no wry face even at the intensely bitter quinine, and when he was done he did not bother to wipe his mouth. A smear of the chlorodyne hung on his lips.

Father Higler stood watching him as he lay back again. There was nothing else that he could do. Philip suffered alone, patiently, and quietly except for an occasional grunt which he could not suppress. Then the priest sat at the end of the bed, still watching as Philip's hurried breath pumped his mid-section rapidly up and down, as his face and limbs twitched with frequent spasms.

After a while he saw no further use in just sitting there. Besides, his stomach was gnawing with hunger. So he rose, stood for a while stroking his beard looking at the servant's twitching eyes and lips, and then covered his lower extremities with a tattered piece of blanket which he spotted on the floor at the end of the bed. Then he took his leave.

'T-a-n-k you F-a-d-a!'

The voice brought him to a startled stop at the threshold of the door. He had thought Philip was asleep. 'All right, Philip,' he said, 'I shall return shortly. I am leaving the medicines behind.'

'Yes Fada.'

He stepped out.

At the mission he warmed some milk and soaked pieces of bread in it for breakfast. Then he sat in the veranda to endure the silence caused by Philip's absence, realizing for the first time that Philip was the biggest constancy in his life, waking him up every morning with the muffled noises of the kitchen, near at hand throughout the day even when he was not in sight. The loneliness which usually only fingered him in those hours before bedtime when Philip had left for the day, now wrapped him in a cold, smothering embrace. For even though it was mid-morning and sunlight was pouring from the sky, it was nevertheless as if everybody had sneaked away and left him behind. The masons were not working. It was the farming season, and the villagers were busy in their farms. Even the sheep were on tethers, therefore not holding their usual session under the mango tree in front of the church.

Finding the silence and solitude unbearable, he rose and walked again to Philip's hut, this time to bring the servant back with him to the mission, lugging him, the black arms of the servant draped limply over the shoulders of the small, freckled, bearded Alsatian priest. The two of them were like soldier and wounded comrade -- the load much bigger than the carrier. But the priest was willing and his heart was stout, even though he had to stop now and then against a tree to catch his breath or adjust the balance between him and his burden.

He encountered two little boys on his way. 'Is he dead?' they asked.

'No,' he replied. 'He is not dead.'

They followed him at a discreet distance, and even though he could not turn to look at them, he could hear their footsteps and their low whispers.

He wished they were bigger – adults – so they could perhaps help him with his burden, but they were children, safely for themselves and unkindly for him, and he had to go on trudging along with his burden, panting from the breath being crushed out of him in the inescapable embrace.

After a while he could bear it no longer. His shoulder bones threatened to crack and his legs to buckle. He fell to his knees against a roadside tree, and rested his burden against it while he recovered his breath. Then he picked it up again and shuffled forward.

He put Philip down on the floor of the parlour on a straw mat, draped his own blanket over him and sat watching over him as his fever burned, much saddened by the illness but glad for the opportunity to serve the servant.

Later that evening he decided to go for a stroll. When he came back, Philip had betaken himself to the kitchen and had made a fire for himself there. He let him be.

And that was how Philip came to live permanently at the mission. He grunted through the first night, audible from the kitchen where he had insisted on sleeping. Once in the middle of the night he cried out in what must have been a nightmare, and Father Higler rose and went flashlight in hand to where he lay on his mat on the dusty kitchen floor. The halo of the flashlight showed him lying on his belly. He squinted out of the corner of his eyes like a dazzled wild animal. Sweat poured off his face.

'Philip!' Father Higler called.

'Yes Fada.'

'How do you feel?'

'Awright.'

Father Higler stood watching. Philip rolled over on his back, shutting his eyes to escape the light. His stomach, despite its bands of muscles, caved into his trunk. One of his hands tightly squeezed a rosary; the other lay a few inches from a recently sharpened broad machete. A bottle of holy water sat at the head of the pallet, and beside it a cup. It seemed that Philip had been drinking the holy water as well as sprinkling it.

After that first night, he seemed to get much better. However, his fever did not burn itself out until after about a week. On two other nights within that time he cried out in his sleep, and Father Higler had to come to his side.

When the fever finally left him, it seemed to have changed him profoundly, to have left his body but not quite his mind. He looked gaunt and many years older than his original self. His face seemed to have sunken deeper, his jaws to have caved in further, and his eyes to have receded farther into his skull. From there they swam in untold mysteries, flaring, bobbing and convulsing. Sometimes they seemed not to focus at all. At other times they appeared to come to a focus behind the object they beheld.

But he did resume the duties of his estate – cooking, washing, and serving – and performed quite well, except that a few slips of carelessness now seemed to have found their way into his previously impeccable service. His hands shook as he poured the tea, and he seemed helpless to control them. Once he knocked over the tea cup and spilled the hot liquid on the priest's lap. Father Higler thereafter decided to excuse him from that particular duty. He could no longer pretend normality. And then there was another anomaly of behaviour – one which would have gone unnoticed in others, but which stood out because Philip was Philip. He was no longer sure to wake up before Father Higler in the morning.

The days wore on. One evening Father Higler stopped Philip in the act of clearing the plates and said: 'Philip.'

'Yes Fada.'

'You remember the day when you fell sick?'

'Yes Fada,' Philip answered.

'I did not mean any harm. Understand? I had only wanted to tell you there was nothing in your life to be ashamed of. Me here,' he tapped his chest, 'I ran away from the war. Would you believe that? I was in the middle of it and I ran away. That is how I came to be a priest. I deserted under fire. Out of fear, cowardice . . .'

'Fada was afraid?'

'For my very life, Philip. That's right, Philip. You see, I too have known despair, as deep as what you now face, or perhaps even deeper. For in the heat of battle I had no time to ponder my decisions and no one to give me advice. I ran, just as you did from your initiation.'

'What did Fada do then? What cure did Fada find for his despair?'

'Hope. One finds a new hope. I found a new hope in the priesthood, in serving God exclusively.'

Philip exhaled, clasped his hands across his chest and wrestled with unspeakable thoughts. 'Fada, Fada is satisfied now? Fada's heart is now in complete peace?'

The question made him want to laugh and cry at the same time. He looked down on the ground before him, then lifted his eyes to Philip's patiently expectant face, shaking his head slowly as he said: 'No, Philip. No . . .'

No indeed, he thought, sighing and shifting in his seat. Not even in a priest's heart did peace pitch its tent for long. Neither the contemplative life nor the journey to Africa nor fervence in prayer procured peace in any large or lasting measure. As he looked up, he found Philip still staring at him. He sighed, and his head began shaking slowly as again he said, 'No, Philip. Peace is only a promise. We have been told there can be no peace on this side of heaven. So it is futile to expect it.'

'Fada, it is truly like that. New hope does not live long before it change to despair. But, but what we do?'

'We still hope. Like little children we trust in God, our only refuge.'

'And the only reward we are promised, Fada, is a happy death, is that not so, Fada? Where is the justice of it?'

'God is the author of all justice. We take what we are given and pray for more. And hope that our pursuits in life, our faiths, prayers and sufferings have not been in vain.'

'We cannot be sure?'

'No, for even in death we stand in danger of God's ominous judgement.'

'And nothing is really up to us?'

'Our salvation is up to us.'

Philip grunted. His mouth twitched, pushing his cheek to one side. Fada had no answers, only distant hopes and promises. His God was like other gods, like the idols and the jujus. So where now? What other God? What other duties and obligations? What other hopes of freedom held before the slave to keep him slaving harder? The horizon that kept moving back and moving back, no way to reach it, no way to come even close to it. One grew old hoping and died still hoping. The hope is pushed back to the other bank of the death-river. And one was not even free to shake one's fist in anger! The gods demanded duty and sacrifice – Fada's God as well as the jujus – but owed nothing. It was not just! One should have at least one choice! One voice! One act that speaks loudly! One act!

But what act would be big enough, heinous enough? Not an indecisive and half-hearted rebellion, but an act that would defy the injustice of this relationship, and stink all the way to Fada's heaven and back again in the heart of the Land. A taboo. An unforgivable mortal sin!

He could not abandon Christianity now and return to the native gods, beg their forgiveness and plead to be accepted back to their slavery. Yet there was no secure shelter for him in Christianity. He was in the middle – no going forward or back, neither up nor down.

Father Higler chuckled mechanically as the servant ambled away. Chewed at the ends of his spectacles. He was a little surprised and appalled that the confession of his desertion on which he had placed so much premium had at last been made with such little impact on himself or on Philip. But it had been made, and that in itself was an accomplishment.

The weeks passed, and Philip continued to live at the mission – a fact that Father Higler first viewed as a departure from normality that would sooner or later return to its appointed state but that in the long run became normality itself. Philip was still loath to share his burdens, and beyond the physical reality of their staying together, there was no confluence of thoughts and no mixing of tears between them. They were like two wounded soldiers caught behind enemy lines, neither of them much help or relief to the other. But Father Higler felt he owed the greater responsibility. Philip had now broken his last ties with his own people and had come to live with him, a refugee, a ward of the faith, his ward.

The servant got better as time went on, but was never quite fully recovered. The lights and shades continued to play in his eyes, occasionally more wildly than at other times. In the meantime, he converted the woodshed into a sleeping room for himself and settled into it. Sometimes he slept there, and other times in the parlour of the rectory. Father Higler would have thought he was fully back to his old self, but for an incident one Sunday evening.

It had been raining that day, and Father Higler had lain down after supper to relax, and without really meaning to, he had fallen asleep. When he awakened and saw no sign of Philip he had gone looking for him with a flashlight, and on pushing open the door of the woodshed, he had found the servant in the middle of a curious ceremony. Philip had built an altar on the floor. An old piece of striped loin cloth was the altar dressing. Two coconut shells holding wax and wick emitted some grey light and filled the room with smoke. A cross of raffia pith leaned on the wall at the centre of the altar. Father Higler would have walked away quietly, had Philip not appeared to be in a trance. He had a bottle of holy water in one hand and was using the other to sprinkle it with abandon to all corners of the room, all the while chanting: 'Leave me alone! Leave me alone! Leave me alone! . . .' His brows were knit with concentration as he threw the water, oblivious of everything around him. His face was covered with sweat.

'Philip!' Father Higler called softly after waiting for a while.

Philip made no response.

The priest shook his head and went away.

12

At long last, the bell arrived at the John Holt Agency, to which his friends in England had consigned it as their contribution to the new church. Father Higler hurried to Aba in a fit of excitement. It was a big bell, worthy of the new church, and he fixed his eyes on it with the awe and joy with which a parent beholds a new infant. He wondered how it would ring. Ah yes, he would soon hear it ringing, no longer far away in his dreams, but soon, tomorrow. He would ring it for the angelus in the morning, at noon and in the evening, for mass on Sunday, for benediction, and, and – and any time he wanted.

'It should ring up everything in the whole blasted bush,' Mr. Barncroft, manager of John Holt, commented.

'Yes,' Father Higler agreed.

'How do you plan to haul it back?'

'That is a problem. I'm not sure. I don't believe a bicycle . . .'

'No, not a bicycle. Maybe a handcart, but not a bicycle.'

'I believe you're right . . .'

When he returned to Saint Peter Claver's late that evening he dispatched word of the good news of his leading parishioners. Arrangements were started to recruit half a dozen young men to accompany him to Aba the second day after, which was a Thursday. They started off just a little after midnight – Father Higler, Philip and the party of young parishioners. Their plan was to load the crate in the rented cart and push in relays as far as the river. Then canoe across.

The trip was tiring, especially since most of the return half was on foot, but Father Higler was garrulous and cheerful and egged the men on with jokes, stories and bad renditions of local work songs. There was a long delay at the river during which an anxious search was made for a canoe sturdy enough to ferry the bell across without too much risk. But then the crossing itself, even though tense, was uneventful.

A large delegation of parishioners was waiting on the other bank, waving and shouting. Father Higler leaped jauntily into knee-deep water and waded into their midst. There were back slaps and enthusiastic hand pumpings. The bell was really there, he told them. And it was big!

For the rest of the journey home, four bicycles were hitched together, side by side and back to back, so that their carriers formed a platform on which the crate was set and securely tied. His parishioners pulled in relays. More people came to meet them as they neared the mission. A procession formed. Men, women and children, Christian and heathen, came out of the clusters of huts to see them, and stood by the roadside waving as if some famous dignitary was passing by. Stooping farmers straightened out and leaned on their hoes to see them pass. The parishioners sang a throaty mixture of work songs, heathen chants and church hymns. When they reached the mission, a volley of dane-gun blasts pre-arranged by the church committee greeted their arrival.

In the gathering dusk, with the sun fallen behind the trees and the river in the distant horizon, and with the forest standing sullenly all around, darkness oozing from its depths, Father Higler and his parishioners laid the crate in front of the hut rectory. Hammer in one hand and chisel in the other, he crossed himself – an example followed by many of those standing around – and began prising the crate open. Cries of 'Uh!' and 'Ah!' issued from many throats long before anyone caught a glimpse of the bell. Then the straw began coming off. 'There it is!' 'I see it!' 'No, you don't!' 'Hold back!' 'Stop pushing!' 'You are making me to fall into Fada!'

And finally there it was, grey, hollow, pear-shaped metal. Father Higler paused in reverent admiration, shook his head, then smoothed a hand over the back of the bell. Then he tapped it lightly with his knuckle, rose to his feet, took one last look at it, then shouldered his way out of the crowd.

He stopped for a visit to his little chapel which was attached to the hut rectory, knelt by the altar and wept tears of gladness.

Early the next morning, the mission was full of people who had come to watch the hoisting of the bell. Philip and Genesis climbed the mango tree in front of the old church and selecting a stout bough, cut it off to leave a stiff projection. The bell was pulleyed towards the stump with heavy climbing ropes, and firmly secured. 'One more wrap!' Father Higler kept saying from the ground. 'How does it look, Philip?'

'Awright, Fada,' Philip replied.

'Give it one more wrap to be sure,' Father Higler said.

Finally he was satisfied that it was secure. The ringing rope went up, and Genesis tied it to one end of the bar. Then counting to three and getting the crowd on their marks and ready, he threw down the other end of the rope. There was a wild scramble for the honour, the immortality, of having been first to ring it. Every man, woman and child converged on the dangling rope as if through it they could reach the kingdom of heaven which had been promised them. Father Higler felt himself bumped from all sides, stepped into the hem of his soutane and fell. He was piqued, but only momentarily. The bell was already ringing. He leaped to his feet, dropped his breviary, and heartily thrust his shoulder into the cluster of outstretched hands, finally rising on his toes before his hand, freckled and white among all the blacks, made contact with a piece of rope.

Every inch of rope within reach was covered by an eager hand. Some held with two hands, others with one, and still others who could not make direct contact with the rope held on symbolically to the hands of others who could. At length their excited chatter subsided as they concentrated their energies and attention on the business of ringing. They synchronized their pulls and acquired a heave-ho rhythm. Up! Down! Up! Down! . . . The bell swung wildly this way and that, whipping its head from side to side like a drunken beast and issuing its call into the wind for miles and miles around, alerting all inhabitants of the villages and the forests, the grounds and the skies to its loud and alien voice.

This was a moment Father Higler had often dreamed about, the highest point so far in his ministry here. And for their part, his parishioners behaved as if they too had been secretly yearning for this occasion. Mesmerized, they pulled rhythmically up and down, up and down, insensitive to everything else except the jangling metallic clangour, which filled their ears, suffused their bodies and reverberated in their hearts.

Church was full the following Sunday. In his sermon, Father Higler talked about the bell, drawing from it a lesson of hope and charity – the charity of his friends in England who had donated it not to him personally but to the parish and all the parishioners. It was their bell. 'And on Sunday morning,' he said, 'when you hear its call, when you hear it saying: "Come! Come! Come!" remember that it is the voice of God calling you to come and worship him. Don't refuse the call, and don't come late . . .

'Now that the bell is here also, it is time for us to start working harder on our new church. We are now like somebody building a house who has the furniture to go in the house when the walls and the roof are not yet complete. Now we have a bell, but it is outside. The sun will be beating on it. The rain will fall upon it. So why don't we resolve to try a little harder, to give one penny more so that our bell can be inside in a place that is worthy of it.'

For several weeks afterwards he rang it at every opportunity, to the limits of reason and then well beyond. Philip for some reason was loath to ring it. Father Higler did not mind; he was only too glad for the opportunity to ring it himself. He rang it so much that when he wasn't ringing it, it reverberated of its own accord in his ears. He would sometimes wake up in the middle of the night thinking he had heard it. He would raise his head from the pillow and listen intently to see if he could hear it again.

The days passed. The rains came in the mornings, afternoons and nights. They came now without preparation or fanfare. The sky simply opened and let the water down, and it was sometimes hard to imagine from where so much water came. When it was not raining the sky was an undifferentiated grey. Sometimes there were swirls of organized clouds in it. Occasionally the sun peeped through an interval, seeming to take the clouds by surprise. If so, they recovered shortly afterwards, and moved to paint out the light. And very soon it rained again.

The rainy season forced idleness and therefore nostalgia on the priest. During the dreary afternoons he would sit on the veranda watching the rain and thinking about himself, his new church, his father, mother, his days in the seminary and his passage to Africa with an old portmaneau which had once belonged to a dead priest. He had used that portmanteau as a seed bed after his arrival. The leather had rotted away, and one day Philip had tried to pick it up and it had collapsed irreparably from the weight of manure in it.

He was truly an orphan, a terminal bud. Perhaps he would never see Europe again, but would die here, and these same rains would drench his grave. The weeds with which he constantly did battle in his garden would get the better of him and grow without restraint over his grave. No, he would ask to be buried under the altar of his new church. He deserved that comfort – please God.

Sometimes the heavy rains drove little holes in the ground and poured from the roof with the sound of frying bacon. Then they set floods of ground water cascading down the pit on the left side of the rectory beyond Philip's Gate, as if a dam had broken. At other times they fell in an endless pat-pat-pattering drizzle, shaking the leaves and making the numerous round puddles of water twinkle like the eyes of a submerged earth monster.

Meanwhile the jungle grew more fiercely green, and its elements struggled to choke and strangle one another. At nightfall it seemed to move in closer, squeezing in around the mission as the darkness descended.

117

The nights were moonless and often starless as well, elementally dark. Mosquitoes raged. Lizards and geckos scurried frightfully up and down the roof.

Philip's behaviour continued to get more eccentric. He shrank farther into himself and farther away from Father Higler who was greatly disappointed that the servant did not care to share with him any of the tumults that raged in his heart. If anything, their living together seemed to have pushed them farther apart emotionally, destroyed the cordiality which had marked their old relationship. Philip was no quieter now than he used to be then; but then his face simply used to be placid. Now the lines of a harsh frown were firmly set on it. His quietness now gave a suggestion of secretiveness, of a purposeful suppression of truth – or if not truth, at least reality. On the other hand, his quietness when Father Higler had first met him had been a true and therefore inoffensive expression of his nature and personality. Father Higler found him a little irritating. The emotional consonance between them seemed jarred. They now seemed to suffer each other quietly because neither could escape the external circumstances that brought and kept them together.

Father Higler was troubled. He felt something was wrong, that something was going to happen to Philip, something like a slow disease was eating him up, wasting away his flesh, thinning his chest and reducing his fingers to bones. Was he going to die?

'Philip,' he called one evening.

'Yes Fada.'

'Come here.'

Philip came, just as of old, but his face was harrowed, his stance less firm, and his total presence less impressive.

'Are you sick?'

'No Fada.'

'No? –' He lifted his eyes briefly into the servant's face. 'Nothing is troubling you? Nothing at all. You don't look too well.'

'I am well Fada.'

'Impossible. You can't be well. Look at you!'

He did not look. But Father Higler did, and noticed a dozen more things to confirm his previous diagnosis.

'Are you happy?'

'Fada, I do not know.'

Father Higler shrugged his shoulders, and asked for a cup of tea. Philip brought it a short time later and then returned to the kitchen where he sat most of the day staring at a wall. He cooked meals and washed plates. He used to teach catechism, but with the rains few people came, and Father Higler was more than happy to handle those himself.

That evening Philip opted for some reason to sleep in the chapel. Father Higler heard some strange noises in the night and rose to investigate. Philip was neither in the woodshed nor in the parlour. Father Higler noticed that the front door to the parlour was unbolted, and his heart began to race. He approached the door cautiously, turned off the light and listened. Nothing. He flung the door open and beamed his flashlight into the darkness of the mission. The chapel door was ajar. Flinging it open and again beaming the light, he found Philip lying under the altar, a machete in one hand and a rosary in the other.

'Philip!' he called out.

'Yes Fada.'

'What are you doing here?'

Philip did not answer.

A sudden anger swept over his puzzlement. 'Get up,' he said. 'This is a chapel, not a place to sleep.'

'Yes Fada,' Philip replied, rose, walked by him back into the parlour where he curled up on the mat like a foetus.

Father Higler was even further puzzled. Try as he might he could not shake off the feeling of impending catastrophe. The present situation could not continue, he thought, without a drastic change for the better or the worse. Worse suggested itself more strongly. Wild thoughts as to what might happen to Philip gnawed at him. He sighed at the servant's apparent suffering, but also at his own helplessness as a man, as a priest.

'Philip,' he was again calling the following day.

'Yes Fada,' Philip replied.

'Tell me, Philip, why don't you get married again?'

Philip stood rigidly frozen where he was, his eyes blinking repeatedly, then seeming to focus on a distant object behind and beyond the priest. His head began shaking slowly in negation.

'No Fada,' he said. 'No marriage.'

'Why not, Philip? One survives and overcomes life's tragedies. Your next marriage might – ought to – work out better. Death . . .' He balked himself on the way to repeating phrases which belonged to Old Man Ahamba.

'What will marriage do for me *now*?'

'It will be a new beginning. It will give you a fresh hope.'

'Fada how can I hope?'

'How can you despair?'

'One enters into hope and comes out in despair.'

'Do not even talk of despair, for it is a sin to despair. Despair is the ultimate negation of almighty God and his providence. A wife would give you companionship and a diversion from yourself. Your life is too narrow now. You should expand it. Get yourself a wife like the rest of the fellows, and maybe some farms. I am a priest and must live the way I do because the Church declares it to be so, but you are a layman. With a wife you will have someone to share your burdens and your joys. A wife and the children God may choose to bless you with.'

'God will give me children?'

'Yes, of course, Philip. Why not? Certainly you don't believe the rubbish some native seers might have said about curses following you from former incarnations. There are no such curses and no such incarnations. As you well know when people die, their souls go to heaven or hell, from which there can be no migration.'

Philip stood thoughtfully, silently.

'Besides you are a man. Do you never have urges for a woman?'

'Fada, fornication is sin.'

'I know, but . . .' The priest was lost for words.

'Fada if I wanted marriage, I would not have the money for the bride price.'

'You wouldn't?'

'No Fada.'

'How much would it cost you?'

'Fada, it depend on the woman and her people.'

'You have nothing at all?'

'No Fada.'

'No?' The priest's brows furrowed, his eyes narrowed. He bit his lips as an unpalatable, bitter thought surfaced on his mind. Why, Oh God? How did this come to be? he thought. 'How long did you work for Father Schlotz?'

'Fada, it was making three years when he get sick.'

'And you have been with me over a year and half. Did Father Schlotz ever pay you anything?'

'No Fada.'

'Fantastic! You mean, you really mean you have worked here for four and half years without pay? My God, why didn't you ask for something? Why didn't you complain?'

Philip shrugged the questions away.

'But why? Why?' Father Higler persisted. 'You certainly deserved something.' He was trying to assuage the feeling of guilt – he felt it should have occurred to him before now to pay Philip – which was swelling his chest. 'You and Father Schlotz never talked salaries at all?'

'No Fada. Fada then had nobody to cook for him permanent. So I cook for him from my own free will. He liked my cooking, so I stay and cook for him.' A shrug as a final punctuation mark.

'That is unbelievable, Philip. I must take steps to rectify that. You have more than earned the money for a bride price from this parish.'

'No need, Fada. I need nothing *now*.'

'The labourer is worthy of his hire.'

'There is no need, Fada. I need nothing *now*.'

Father Higler sighed.

Philip waited for a few moments, then walked away.

Three days later Genesis' wife delivered. She had some difficulties in her labour, but ultimately she gave birth to a bawling, bouncy baby girl.

'A girl again?' Genesis wondered. Had God forgotten what he needed?

'Another girl?' the villagers commented.

Happiness with alloys. Praise God regardless. Count blessings rather than misfortunes.

The little girl was named Onyenmachi, 'Who-Knows-What-God-Is-Thinking?' Who knows?

13

'Philip?'

There was no answer.

'Philip!' he called again insistently.

Still no answer.

Father Higler startled himself into wakefulness and was now at a loss to explain the apparent alarm in his voice. It was not usual for him to call for Philip while he was yet in the bedroom. As he gained more control over his faculties, he realized that he had slept late. The light that oozed into the room from the chinks where the walls met the slope of the roof was the hardened light of mid-morning, not the wan glow of dawn. He could not remember having turned even once in his sleep during the night.

He shuffled into the parlour, opened the back door and looked towards the kitchen. 'Philip!' he called again, singing the name. No answer. 'H'm, I wonder . . .' he said, and ambled back to the bedroom and put on a pair of shorts. There was no fire in the kitchen, and no sign that there had been once since the night before. The side gate through which Philip came and went most of the time was open. It gave no clues. The basin on the wash-stand contained the murky water in which he had washed his hands when he finished working in the garden the evening before. The dirt had settled neatly to the bottom. He picked the basin up and flung the water away, then walked to the water pot where with a can he measured several cups of water into the basin. He soaked his face and shaved the edges of his beard.

A strange feeling of bereavement encompassed him. There was really no reason for alarm because it was already mid-morning and Philip could have gone to the well, or church or any of a dozen places. Yet he found it hard to suppress the misgiving that something serious was amiss.

He opened the front door and stood in front of the veranda like one mesmerized. A yawn. He stared blankly in front of him across the empty space of the mission, until his vision collided with the familiar but impenetrable face of the forest. He yawned again, feeling drowsy, and stretched himself, creaking at several joints. He felt like going back to bed. 'But I just got out of bed!' he thought fretfully. 'I must have a bit of malaria coming.' In that case, the best thing would be to try to walk it off. He began walking towards the road. Arriving there he stopped and looked both ways, as perchance he might see Philip returning. But Philip wasn't anywhere to be seen. In the surrounding forest insects were sniping, squirrels hopping and birds chirping. A mild breeze stirred the leaves. Surface phenomena, comouflaging an interior where neither his vision nor his imagination could penetrate.

He felt hungry.

Where in blazes had Philip gone, anyway? His mind pursued a number of false leads, but finally wound up at the position nought. Then it occurred to him that he had not looked in the woodshed where Philip slept. He might be curled up in a corner there, dead. He hastened to the woodshed and examined every nook. But there was no Philip. A rosary, a broad machete, a neatly furled mat and a bottle of holy water were all he found, a representative coat of arms for Philip in his recent state. The only unusual item in the whole room was the Saint Christopher medal which he found in the dust on the floor. Its normal place was on a string around Philip's neck. He picked it up and examined it, even sniffed it for a hint of blood. No hints. He balled up the broken string and put it in his pocket.

Had Philip gone back home? . . . Hardly. But even then, he should be at the mission during the day. That was the natural order of things . . . He would find out by going to his compound. But after donning his soutane he changed his mind and decided to cook breakfast for himself first.

He felt a chill as he stood in the dark kitchen. The fireplace was cold. The three-legged iron cooking stand stood over half-burned wood and a heap of ash – cold ash – and it was impossible to tell when a fire had last been there. He kicked a toe into the ash to see if there were any warm embers. Then he waved his hand over the ash, finally touching the iron stand. It was perfectly cold. He exhaled and looked around.

The kitchen smelled of Philip the way a shrine smelled of a god. His essence permeated the place. He was in the air, and the walls and the roof, in the bucket and the dirty water in it, in the unwashed plates from last night's supper. Strange, he thought. Philip ordinarily never left plates unwashed overnight. This was like a dead man's room after the burial – the half-eaten coconut drying into copra in the corner of the fireplace, the whiff of snuff. It made him recall his father's room after his death, the characteristic incidentals such as the muddy boots never to be worn again, the soiled handkerchief, the carefully folded tobacco wrapper, the half-smoked pipe. He exhaled and went out and stood in front of the kitchen door and scanned the surroundings, seeing the tops of the palm trees waving in the breeze and the immovable jungle beyond the back fence – seeing them, as far as he could recall, for the first time from what had been Philip's regular point of view.

He would say mass, he thought, say it slowly and consume most of an hour. And that would be an hour less to worry about. Or perhaps by the time he finished Philip would have returned. His mind wanted to advance the day, to rush it forward, ostensibly towards darkness and bedtime. But he realized that time would be just as meaningless in darkness as in light if Philip were not to return. He understood then, in small measure, the timeless sense of the natives, their disinclination to quantify or demarcate time, an attitude of mind which made speed irrelevant.

No! He sighed with sudden irritation. He would not say mass today. As a priest, he had an obligation to say mass daily. But he would not say mass today. Why was his life a series of obligations?

He ambled back to the parlour and removed his soutane, then returned to the kitchen to make a fire. He shoved the ashes aside and built the pieces of wood to a head, then struck a match. No fire resulted from his effort. He often thought of himself as being made of pioneering material. Lighting this fire was more than enough test for his talents; for after more than half an hour and after most of the contents of a valuable box of matches had been spent, there was still no fire. He walked outside beyond Philip's gate to the edge of the forest and picked up some twigs. They burned up quickly but the fire did not catch on the larger pieces of wood. He sniffed some of the bottles he found leaning into one of the nooks of the kitchen. One of them contained kerosene, which he poured generously over the wood. It flared on being lighted, catching the edges of his beard and causing him to leap to his feet in apprehension. But in a few moments the fuel had burned out, and still the robust pieces of wood remained unimpressed. Sweating, bleary-eyed and covered with soot and ash, he stumbled outside.

His pocket watch said ten to twelve, time for the noon angelus. He rang the angelus and prayed it. At the end, the thought occurred to him that perhaps if he rang the bell long enough and loudly enough, Philip would hear him and return from wherever he was. Or perhaps some of his parishioners would come to learn the reason for the bell's call.

What would happen if he never saw Philip again?

The thought caused him to shudder, for whatever – if anything – had happened to Philip could easily happen to him. In the far-flung reaches of these forests he could gasp his last, flutter to stillness and be laid to rest under an obscure bush. He felt small, lost and afraid. The noon sun now at its zenith directly overhead cast him in his proper size, a small circular patch of shadow, hardly a significant punctuation mark in the face of this vast jungle – Africa, the world, the sky, the infinitude of God's space, the eternity of his time. The finite attempting to arrest the infinite! To gather the oceans of the world in a cup! The mountains in the palms of one's hands!

'God, what can I do?' he muttered in a manner reminiscent of Philip. And he wondered whether God's answer would be like his to the servant. 'Nothing. There is nothing to do. Nothing can be done.'

He entered the chapel the way the village old men entered the fetish hut to consult their gods. Meditate. Contemplate the unsolved mysteries of his existence, his mission, his salvation. Philip's mysterious absence. Would it not be better to get himself something to eat first? Hunger was such a bad ally to prayerfulness. No. The chapel was in darkness. The sanctuary lamp had been extinguished. Had he not told Philip the evening before – yes, he had, he could remember very well telling Philip – to pour some kerosene into the lamp. He went back into the house to get a match. Struck a flame into the twilight.

'God!'

An abomination!

Heinous sacrilege!

The tabernacle had been ripped off its supports and splintered across the altar table. The *ciborium* lay on the floor. White circular wafers of Sacred Host lay all around on the floor, where it appeared they had been trampled. The crucifix had been broken to matchsticks.

God!

Shaking, Father Higler returned to the rectory to fetch the large hurricane lamp. He held up the lamp and peered fearfully, still shaking, still uncomprehending. Philip had gone mad. But what sort of madness? Was that the only direction in which his madness could move him? He set the lamp down, knelt down on the kneeler in front of the desecrated altar and pillared his knuckles under his chin. But he could not pray. He could not think. He did not know what to pray for or what to think. He crossed himself, genuflected and began gathering the Sacred Host and consuming it. Then he walked hurriedly from the chapel as if it contained a fearful thing.

It was quiet outside, placid and peaceful. The only crisis was in his heart. Find Philip. Find him, and have an accounting. If he could still be found. If the vengeance of almighty God had not reached out and struck him down already! His footsteps directed him to Philip's original compound, but he digressed briefly to look at the old church. Nothing was amiss there, and Philip was not there.

The compound was quiet and peopled exclusively by little children on this afternoon, not a normal situation, for this was not the peak of the farming season. A cluster of children under the shade trees, a slightly older girl supervising their play. They did not greet him with the burst of excitement and questions which he had learned to expect from most of the children of the village. Instead they fell to sudden silence on his approach.

'Where are your fathers and mothers?' he inquired.

They all shook their heads as if they had been practising the art. The older girl spoke. 'We do not know,' she said.

'They did not tell you where they were going?'

'No,' she repeated. 'We do not know anything.'

'You do not know anything,' Father Higler repeated and then swallowed. 'You see Philip today?'

'No.'

He looked at the children and sighed, opened his mouth to speak again but changed his mind and walked instead to Philip's door. A padlock was fixed on it and locked. He stared for some moments. Then on an impulse he called out: 'Philip!'

There was no answer. There shouldn't have been, for Philip himself had put that padlock there when months before he had moved to the mission. But he called again, 'Philip! Philip! ...'

There was still no answer, except from a dog which sat with the children. It started barking at him. The children themselves huddled together and stared at him with the silent mystification of startled sheep. He turned around and left them.

It was now past mid-afternoon and the sun was falling towards the river. His misgivings about Philip were fast turning into suspicions that the servant had come to no good end. But he could not understand the wreckage of the chapel. He stopped by Matthew's compound, but Matthew was not at home and nobody there had seen Philip or heard anything about him. Genesis was not at home either. No men were at home anywhere. The entire male population seemed to have gone off to a secret war.

But just before he turned into the mission, he encountered Old Ahamba.

'Ah, my White friend,' he called out. 'How is your health today?'

'Uncertain. How is yours?'

'I endure my aches without grunting, seeing that both life and death are equally painful. But you hurry. Where have you been?'

'I am looking for Philip.'

'Ah, your pot boiler.'

'Yes. Have you seen him?'

'There is little I have not seen in my long survival. But yes, there are a few things. A few things yet there must be.'

'I am hardly in the mood for riddles.'

'Ah, how is your mood? You look troubled.'

'Good afternoon, Ahamba. We can chat another time. I must find Philip, and I am hungry.'

'Come,' Ahamba said, laying a hand on his shoulder.

'Why?'

'Because I have called you. Come to my house. If it is food you want, I have more than one wife who can satisfy any man's taste. Does your religion forbid you to eat woman's cooking?'

'No, why?'

'It is a man that cooks for you, and so I was wondering. Exalted states of life have their disciplines. Me, for instance, as *dibia*, I am forbidden to eat anything touched by a woman during her monthly bloom.'

Father Higler pulled a watch out of his pocket. 'I must return to the mission and ring the angelus first.'

They walked to the mission together in the waning light, priests of different gods, different ages and different lights. The mission was quiet, almost desolate. If Philip had been there, smoke would have been trailing skywards from the kitchen and the beat of pestle against mortar would have punctuated the silence. Now there was just the unbroken silence.

He rang some of it away with the clangour of the angelus. The Old Man asked for explanations. There was no way to explain briefly, and Father Higler felt too tired to embark on the long project. But he had little choice. So he told in sketches the story of the conception of Christ by the Holy Spirit.

'This god was born by a woman who did not cross legs with a man?'

'Yes.'

'And he was really god and man at once and people saw him?'

'Yes.'

'Then what happen?'

'He was murdered by his people.'

'Ah yes, I remember now. The happy sufferer.'

The loud boom of an overloaded dane-gun exploded in the area of the forest known as Ogwugwu.

'*Ihem!*' the old man ejaculated, circling his hand ritually around his head and snapping his fingers. 'I wonder who is shooting what?'

They walked along in silence. 'You know,' the old man said after some time. 'Those bushes over there so thick, you know why they are called Ogwugwu? . . . I tell you . . .'

He began a story which he told with fervour. It was obviously a legend with a few real physical corroborations, but even these had been so interpreted as to give them supernatural dimensions, when, in fact, they were thoroughly mundane. Ogwugwu, he said, meant Deep Hollow. Long ago it had been the bed of a lake – the Treacherous Lake of the Seven Whistling Devils. The founder of the village had warred against the Devils

127

and vanquished them. The lake had dried up. The founder had wanted the river which joined with it to stay, but the river wanted '*Male* and *Female*' in sacrifice. The founder would not think of offering a son and a daughter, and so the river went elsewhere. It was not until after the river had gone that the founder went to a seer only to find out that what the river had actually wanted was a male and female chameleon. Legends, Ahamba admitted. But in our legends we remake ourselves, crawl out of the shells that imprison us and grow larger.

'Have a seat, White man,' the old man said to Father Higler. 'As my father say when he lived, a small matter can be talked standing up, but big matter can take four days. Or even eight. Have seat.'

Father Higler sat on one of the low wooden stools, the one nearest the door so that whatever breeze came into the place would hit him first and directly. He disposed himself for a great deal of circumlocutious talk, most of which would be lost on him in the endless proverbs the old man insisted on using. The room was characteristically windowless and caught in semi-darkness, but he knew that the sun would have to be completely down before Ahamba lighted a lantern. Meanwhile the latter continued to talk and stare at him, while he himself listened as best he could and stared around languidly. The shadows outside grew long and ghostly, the atmosphere tired. Two of the largest *uha* trees on the compound were aerial cities for weaver birds which had returned from the day's forage and were engaged in continuous chatter. They reacted to the occasional outbursts of the children with concerted outbursts of their own.

Ahamba kissed a kola nut and offered it to the priest. He broke it according to custom, kept two cotyledons for himself and returned the other two to the old man. He demurred on the pepper seeds.

'Thank you for kola,' he then said. 'But you must tell me, have you seen Philip?'

Ahamba chuckled without amusement. 'Those who know do not say . . . That is a saying we have.'

'I am well aware of that, and I think it is a very clever saying, but have you seen Philip? Do you know where he is or what has happened to him?'

'It is your intention to draw the lie from my mouth?'

'The truth . . . You have seen Philip then. Is he alive?'

'He lives to the sorrow – the horror – of all of us.'

'He is alive then. Is he mad? What has happened to him? What has he done?'

'Something that is not done! Something the Land forbids. Something painful to recount. But you must eat first. We do not have your kind of food, but I have heard you have a good appetite for eggs. Eggs are boiling for you . . . Come with me.'

They stepped outside into the twilight, past the animal shelters, towards a grove of trees where the fetish huts and major juju shrines were located.

'You have answers for me, I presume,' Father Higler said wearily.

'Me?' Ahamba said, slapping his chest. 'No. No answers. I have only questions. A few answers I have are only for myself. No, I have nothing to lay down and prescribe. How can I? How can anyone? I can vouch only for the experience that has been mine. Which is one reason I am surprised at you. You seem to claim to have answers for others as well as for yourself. Tell me, how did you become a priest? . . .'

'You would like to hear the story of my life? It is too long for one evening, too involved to relate on an empty stomach and at a time like this. I chose to become a priest, and then again I was chosen in that I believe I had a vocation, a calling, a voice summoning me to duty.'

'Duty. Ah yes, we are summoned to duty always, are we not? Your pot boiler too? He too was summoned to duty but defected. And now *this*.'

'*This*? What *this* are you talking about? What has Philip done? Please, please . . .'

He broke off. His bowels gurgled from their emptiness. The Old Man moved on from where they had paused before the first juju shrine.

'Do you find it a burden, the life of a priest?'

'Yes-s-s,' he said reluctantly, and therefore heavily. 'It has its demands, but the rewards are higher.'

'That is good. A man should not slave for nothing and labour in vain. Rewards. Are there rewards also for those from here who have joined you? Your pot boiler?'

'Yes. For everyone in the state of God's grace.'

'Mmmh,' Ahamba grunted. 'Conditions are attached only to rewards. There are no conditions on duties that bind. But who is the author of these promises, these expectations which you cherish? The god-man who was hanged on a tree?'

'Yes. Jesus Christ in heaven is the author of the Christian promise. The guarantor and guardian. God himself who neither deceives nor is deceived.'

'And your surety? What is your condition in the bargain?'

'None. One does not bargain with the Almighty. Faith is our only guarantee. Faith that God will be faithful to his promises.'

'Is he?'

'Yes. Inasmuch as we are able to understand his promises and his biddings.'

'In my youth, I too was a man of faith in all these jujus and idols. That faith gave me hope. The hope later gave me despair. But I have to go past despair to a new understanding. You see this here?' He pointed to a clay figurine in the likeness of a prolific, motherly woman, with exaggerated busts and bosoms. 'That is my *Edo*, the goddess of fruitful womanhood. My wives and daughters as well as my sons' wives have all been fruitful. So I am happy and *Edo i*s happy. She gets all her sacrifices regularly, and they are generous because she is generous. The right hand washes the left hand and the left hand washes the right hand, and both hands are happily washed. That there is the hut of my *Amadioha*, god of the thunders and rainstorms. He delights in rattling his anger. He is powerful and he is wrathful. Look over there. Last year he smashed down a coconut tree in the middle of my compound. I grunted and then let him know that I would comply with his wishes, but I would not cower indefinitely. There was a point beyond which my fear would not drive me. He was threatening to kill my first son, so the seers said. "Protect him instead!" I said to it, "for if anything happens to him, I will burn down your hut and bury you!" I gave it sacrifices. My sons are well and prosperous . . . And that low hut there, you see it, with all the wooden idols? Those are my *Agwu*. They are peevish and always a nuisance. They make trouble for you if you offend them, not big trouble but bundles of little mischief. You hurt your finger, fall and break your leg, they push you and your children into accidents. I have not repaired the roof of their hut for more than one year, so when it rains, it rains on them. And they know that I am not bluffing because they are not the first set I have owned. They are the third! The first set I threw out to the termites. The second fared even worse. In anger one day, I made them into a pile, took my prick like this and pissed in their eyes. I called my children and together we made water all over them. And then I burned them . . .

'But it gets dark, and you are hungry. Come, let us go back to the eggs. Just know that there is no lack of gods here. We make them ourselves. In other villages, there are other gods, just as it is where you come from. We create our own gods to guide, rule and protect us. Mine drove me to the brink of madness in my youth. In age I have learned to buck their tyranny. And that, my friend, has been my conquest of despair, negotiating a new understanding with all these gods.'

'I imagine given the chance you would like to convert me to your kind of juju worship,' Father Higler said as they now retraced their steps to the centre of the compound.

'Convert you? Why should I want to convert you? What advantage to

130

me? I hold no commission from anyone, god or man. What I have told you is the story of my *own* life, not an example or prescription for anyone else to follow. I do not proselytize my way of life. Do you not remember our other conversations? I cannot ask you to have a haircut like mine because our faces are not alike. . . .'

A youngish wife brought Father Higler six boiled eggs in a wooden bowl, three peeled and salted, three not.

'Thank you,' he said and fell on the eggs.

'Your pot boiler has done something that is not done.'

'What has he done?'

'And I wonder what made him to do it?' I told you when the gods are after you, they come after you in devious ways. A man should not challenge a gorilla to a wrestling match unless he has made sure of his own strength.'

'What has Philip done?'

'Do you have any offences in your land for which a man pays with his life?'

'Murder? Has Philip killed somebody?'

'In some ways worse.'

'Please stop the riddles and tell me what he has done!'

'Ah, do not get angry at me. You need friends. You need my friendship tonight at the judgement.'

'Look, my man, will you tell me what Philip has done, where he is, what is happening to him? You should see what he did to my chapel. Has he gone mad?'

'It would have been better if his head had lost its correctness. Your pot boiler, White Man my friend, has crossed legs with his own daughter. The mindless one they call Ugochi, you know her.'

'Impossible! What are you saying?'

'I am saying nothing.'

'Philip would not do a thing like that. This is not something some seer has told you?'

'He was seen.'

'Someone saw Philip commit the act?'

'And he has not denied it himself.'

Father Higler bolted to his feet speechless, half an egg in his hand, the other half stuck to his gullet like a morsel of plaster.

14

An islet of dismembered forest next to a grove of ancient trees – *apu* trees with umbellate branches spread like hands in supplication to the low-hanging sky. The moon was missing, but there were the older stars, faded and flickering like dying flames. Only the old men were here tonight, the very old – juju priests and the *dibia* set and the *isi oparas* from each of the village kindreds – scrolls of wisdom – strongest links with the past – tabloids of tradition, distinguished by the length of their survival and the good fortune of having joined the procession of generations before their living relatives – weak, withered bodies embodying the longest memories of the village. They milled around like half-naked demons in the brown light of the *owa* torches, amidst the quivering shadows of the forest and the haphazard flights of moths and winged termites driven by the death urge towards the crackling flames – all in this ancient concourse used only on the rarest and most momentous occasions.

'White Man,' Old Man Ahamba was now saying, 'how do you justify yourself at times like these?'

Father Higler did not reply. His mind, like a mouth chockful of food, could not churn on its contents.

'We do,' Ahamba continued. 'We try. We bind ourselves to all the justice we are capable of and we stake our survival on it. We must. That is our way ... I go now.'

And he went, towards a tree where some others had gone before him, circled an egg ritually around his head, muttered his *ogus*, incantations of justification, tossed the egg against the tree and then watched the spilled contents dribble slowly to the ground.

Grunts. Suppressed coughs. Kola nuts and pepper seeds pass from hand to hand. Horn tips filled with tobacco snuff exchanged. The musty whiff of age grown careless about bodily hygiene, age neighbourly with death. Skins of wrinkled leather. Shiny skulls. Empty, blue gums. The tiny but hoarse tinkle of the *ogele* – king-kong, king-kong, king-kong. The muffled and mysterious grumblings of the forest.

'I do not remember the last time a meeting was held here. But my father told me about it. It was the night before our village went to war with Amafor. I was young then. Ah, to think of the valour associated with that war and then with what we do here tonight . . . Feats of valour we honour with a parade around the market. A man is carried on the shoulders for all to see. He is celebrated with singing and dancing and pleasure. But what we do tonight is *ikwu umi*. The blood of this village has been poisoned. The bad blood must be let . . . Do such things as this ever happen in your home tribe? What do you do? . . . You do not speak. You are speechless from your crowded thoughts. My pity. But do you know why he did it?'

That was the question Father Higler had been asking over and over in his mind. Why? Why, Oh God, why? We have our memories, our imagination, our wills and our intellect, but what we have is so tightly hemmed and circumscribed, and we are constantly reminded of what we do not have and held at bay by our deficiencies. For an understanding, Oh God, an inkling of an understanding, an intellect to unravel, organize and *understand* the chaos and incongruity in which we are immersed!

This wilderness enough, Oh God! And out of these depths my needs cry out loudly enough! Are we not children of the Promise and the Kingdom? Are not the insoluble mysteries for them that are without? . . .

'Has Philip spoken at all?'

'Profanities. He has sown them in all the winds. He has had a chance to defend himself and will have more. . . . Ah, here they are now – a sight that offends the eye, a man and his own daughter. It makes the body to shudder and shrink back on itself and the blood to curdle and turn cold in its branched and winding channels.'

Philip, stripped of all his clothes, was led into the clearing with his foster daughter and partner in sin. Their heads were shaven and painted with sacrificial blood. Their hands were bound. Father Higler started on seeing them and took a step forward.

'Do not leave your place, White Man,' Ahamba cautioned. 'We are not in a cordial mood tonight!'

Philip looked around the crowd unabashedly, casually, his face placid, his eyes quiet and remorseless. He saw Father Higler but in no wise acknowledged the master.

Why? Philip, why? Father Higler thought, but Philip's eyes did not yield an answer. He wore the same old face which had often puzzled him, the same broad, squat features which volunteered little information to the outsider. And then there was the foster daughter and partner in incest, with dull doe eyes, droopy lips, and fleshy bosom.

Old Man Ahamba continued his earnest whispers. Explanations. Justifications. The Land is greater than all other gods. Greater even than the sky-god, because when the sky cannot any longer hold its rains, it releases them to the Land to hold. And the Land is everywhere. We come from it, we live on it, we return to it. We reincarnate from it. We are always standing on it or on something that stands on it, whether we are on top of a tree on top of water. The rivers and the seas have the Land to hold them up . . .'

A wizened man walked into the centre of the clearing, and punching his hand into the air exclaimed:

'*Teeeeh!*'
'*Ha!*' the assembly answered.
'*Teeeeh!*'
'*Ha!*'
'*Kele nu!*'
'*Ha!*'
'*Nma nma nu!*'
'*Ha!*'

'I saw them,' the man said. 'I was the one who saw them. I saw them with these two eyes in my head here.' He pointed to each eye in turn. 'I swear that I saw them by this *Mgbara Ala*, this *Nne Nchetara*, this *Nne Miri* . . . this *Akwuga*, this *Ekwesu Ntakakpa*, this *Kamanu*, this *Ihi Njoku* . . .' He proceeded to invoke by name all the numerous jujus that were assembled. 'I saw them enter the bush near the Nameless Tree. That was where I saw them. If I did not see them may I fall dead right here on my feet. If I did not see them may all these jujus that are here this night be on my tail throughout all of my reincarnations. On top of a wine tree was where I was when I saw them. I said to myself, "They are father and daughter. They are going somewhere together. Perhaps to the farm to reap cassava." So I continued to climb my palm tree was what I did. Then I looked around when I did not hear their noise anymore. Amadioha strike me blind! What my eyes saw my mouth hesitates to say. Strike me down all of these jujus that are here tonight if what I say I saw I did not see. This him here!' He lunged suddenly forward like a fencer making a thrust, pointing at Philip. Philip stood quietly against the tree whose bark had been carved off and his partner in sin stood beside him. His eyes were cast to the ground, unmoving, unblinking, showing neither distress nor regret. He looked as if he found everything around him boring – his judges, his accuser, the rituals they were performing. Had the Devil taken complete control of the man? Father Higler wondered. Not even the slightest hint of compunction.

'It pained my heart,' the accuser continued. 'I tell you, it pained my heart to see a man fixed to his own daughter. I can see the frowns on your faces now, but you are just hearing about it. Think of me then who saw it. How it pained my heart. I let out a yell, and they saw me and disconnected. By the time I got there they had gone away. I would have cut off his head before saying anything to him, and I would have asked you and the Land to be my judges about what I did . . .'

'What do you think?' Old Ahamba asked the priest.

'Mmmh,' was all Father Higler could manage to answer, a deep, hollow-chested grunt.

'You do not think he did it?'

Father Higler turned a blank gaze at Old Ahamba, but his eyes, his thoughts, were elsewhere, far, far away, his mind still scuttling around for the meaning of *this*. Why? If this was not an act of personal perversity, if Philip had not fallen in a moment of weakness, then why had he done it? Had he gone mad?

'He did it,' Old Man Ahamba said. 'If I did not think he did it, you would have heard me. We are just.'

'*Kele nu!*'

'*Ha!*'

'*Nma nma nu!*'

'*Ha!*'

'*Kwenu!*'

'*Ha!*'

There were greetings and speakers, sowing syncopated eloquence in the night breezes, noting the enormity of Philip's deed – how their eyes hesitated to behold the pair, their ears revolted to hear the deed, and their mouths balked at speaking it. They were not there to deliberate and judge. Guilt was not in doubt. What had to be done should be done quickly, so that the whole episode could be concluded, forgotten, banished from all memory.

'You know,' one man was now saying, 'before the White Man came, it was wrong for a man in this village to go in with a woman in the day time. Now the young men do it. The White Man did not ask them to do it, but they do it because of his coming. Our nights have been turned into days and our days into nights. It seems we are confused. Our old certainties seem no longer to be certified. Strangers argue with our truths, and we stand and stare about like foreigners in our own land – as if we have to ask permission to be who we are and think what we have always thought, and act as our fathers acted before us. The D. O. at Aba wants us to pay him tokens, as if he owns us. We have to justify ourselves to him, and not to our customs, our gods and our traditions, which go beyond memory. But all that is another matter . . . What I am saying is: In the old days, if a man pierced a woman who was his cousin by his great-great-great- – uncountable, but rememberable grandmother, so that only the tiniest drop of blood made them brother and sister, he would have his instrument and his ears cut off, so that the Land would be appeased. But for a man, a man of this village whose navel-tree grows on our soil, who shares our blood pool . . . His own daughter! I will not say it! I find it too gruesome to say. I just wish to ask: What are we waiting for? Has the sun not already set twice since this act? Do we want the anger of the Land on our heads before we act, the anger of the concord of jujus assembled here? Do we want the ground to shake? Or the hills to vomit fire first? . . . I take my seat!'

'Let us make haste and appoint a jury.'

'Why? Is this a judgement? Are there two sides, an accusation and a plea? Are we not all on the same side?'

'The night is deep.'

'Yes, we must not be caught here by the cock's first crow.'

Ahamba: 'Let *him* speak.'

'Speak?'

'But why? Does he have a defence? Must we not do what we must do?'

Ahamba: 'Yes, we do what we must do – sometimes only what we must do. Let him speak. Let him justify himself.'

'Justify?'

'Justify!'

Ahamba: 'Yes, if he can . . . Speak!' he ordered Philip. 'Let the night winds, the hovering spirits of our ancestors, these hallowed forests and trees, this assemblage of gods, the moon, sky and stars and this sacred soil from which we all derive – speak that they may all hear you. Justify yourself. Justify your life – your death is already more than justified. Why should life have been wasted on you? Why should your mother not have closed her legs and crushed your head at your birth instead of opening them wide and letting you out? Yes, why was there rejoicing at your birth, singing and dancing about a new life, when there better should have been mourning and weeping?'

Philip: 'I did not ask to be born!'

136

'Ha! Who did?'

'Is not life the same *favour* done to all of us?'

Philip: 'It was foisted on me. I had no choice in the matter.'

Ahamba: 'On all of us then. But we still do our best with what we get. No one is exempt from the tears of life, from the first one when we swallow the world's breath for the first time, to that last one that wets the straw mat on which we breathe our last. But like river swimmers, do we not launch our hopes ahead of us in the current and swim after them and try to overtake them?'

Philip: 'The hopes after which I swim in the past cannot be counted. All of them false. So I have left hope far behind me. I have no use for hope now.'

'You were not mad then?'

'Your head was correct when you did *this*?'

Philip: 'My torments are worse than madness.'

'Your torments? You mean your cowardice?'

'The escapee must keep on escaping?'

'Yes, the fugitive wins no reprieve from his flight. He unsettles the forest and awakens more pursuers.'

'Right! The correct choice is not to run.'

Philip: 'And that is the choice I have made now!'

'*This!* You chose *this*? *This* is your choice?'

'Profanity. He offends the very air into which he breathes.'

'Pour some punishment on him!'

There was the whine of reed whips through the air, the split-splat of their fall on Philip's bare skin. The girl is spared. Philip does not cry out or even wince. His eyes do not flinch. Only the skin twitches reflexively at the administration of punishment.

'Why are you not remorseful?'

'Why is your tongue quick and at the ready to speak?'

'Do you not know what we must do to you?'

Philip: 'Yes. And I am ready. I have no fear in my heart. But for whose sake must you do it?'

'All. For the sake of all. You. The gods. The Land. All these jujus. Ourselves and our customs and traditions, the whole communion of our group, both living and dead, born and unborn. We have all been tainted by you. The Land must be propitiated with your blood because you have tainted it. It must be cleansed and renewed.'

Philip: 'But why? Because you fear punishment? Then it is you who are afraid. It is you whose hearts shake and tremble. But me, I am not afraid of how you judge me or what you do to me. I have hit my one blow. I have my revenge against everything!'

'Coward! You ran the night of your initiation.'

'Why must he be allowed to gabble on? Why do we not do what we must do?'

Ahamba: 'Let him be yet. The gods are hearing him same as we. They must know we are in no way to blame for him.'

'Maybe, but he offends with every breath, and we are to blame for allowing him to breathe on.'

Philip: 'Ah, now who is the coward? Whose heart trembles with fear?'

'You are not afraid of death?'

Philip: 'No!'

'Why then did you flee the night of your initiation?'

Philip: 'I was afraid then.'

'And becoming a juju priest after your uncle?'

Philip: 'I was afraid then.'

'And you are not fearful now?'

'You are not even fearful of death?'

Philip: 'No.'

'Whence your new courage?'

Philip: 'Did I choose to be born? I was born a slave to duty. I had no choice and no voice. My pains and sufferings, my sweats and tears did not justify me. So I have given myself one choice.'

'And *this* was it? This heinous act! I say enough!'

The interrogator leaped forward and grabbed a machete.

'If he does not stop talking I will behead him here in front of all of you!'

The dramatic gesture brought the interview to a halt.

'Prepare,' was heard around the assembly.

Father Higler stepped forward. 'Gentlemen, I must ask you to spare him.'

'Spare him!'

'Is the White Man crazy?'

'Does he know where he is?'

'Who brought him here in the first place?'

'Ahamba! You are to blame, Ahamba, for any trouble he may cause us. You are his friend.'

Ahamba: 'He will cause us no trouble.'

'He may betray us to the D. O.'

'Betray is a foul word. Are we a conspiracy? Is what we are doing really a secret? Whose law can we offend on our own grounds?'

'The White Man will go to Aba and tell the D. O. and he will come here with *sojas* and police.'

'If the D. O. comes here and says it is good conduct for a man to mount his own daughter, we can ask him if his father did it to his sisters.'

'And he can imprison us, the whole village, with our children and our wives.'

'Yes, we are in this together.'

'Were we ever apart?'

'If we want we can make sure the Fada never reaches Aba.'

'What do we do with him?'

'Many a man has been lost and was never heard from again. We can always say he left our village and went somewhere else, we do not know where.'

'Let us swear him to secrecy on all of these powerful jujus assembled here . . .'

Father Higler: 'Gentlemen, gentlemen, you have not answered my request.'

A man walked up to him and slapped him on the back with the flat side of a broad machete, brushed the sharp tip across his nose. 'Is that enough answer for you? It is perhaps your strange god that drove him into this. And now you want us to spare him. You are lucky to be spared yourself.'

Father Higler: 'Please, please, I beg you! Forgive him. The quality of mercy . . .'

Philip: 'I need no forgiveness! I ask for none!'

'A thing like *this* is not up to us to forgive.'

'And you have heard him.'

Father Higler stepped back, head lowered, hand under his chin, mind reeling.

'Proceed. Prepare to do it,' were heard around the assembly. The old men huddled together, unbagged their *Ofo* sticks and began the rituals of binding themselves into one.

Father Higler looked briefly at Philip and then at the old men. Everything seemed vague and rarefied – the men, the night, the lights, the forest, his thoughts – they all seemed more like mystic intensifications of a bad day dream and less like reality. He had now gone from nadir to nadir through the zenith of an illusory hope. Cowardice in battle, fear in the face of imminent death, could they by any alchemic trick be turned into virtue, and could an apostleship arising therefrom ever attain ennoblement? What about faith then? And the thousand hopes that, according to Ahamba, we launched before us? And the Promise? And the call to follow Me? The priestly cloak offered no immunity? Heaven was no nearer here or now than there or then? God was just as mysterious, just as unobligated, man just as helpless and hapless?

He thought of his passage from Europe on the Elder Dempster steamer, *Obong of Kalabar*, and saw himself – dimly, as if through a dark glass – on the second day after the ship had pulled out of Southampton on its way towards Africa. He had stood on the deck to the portside, then changed to starboard to get out of the wind. That tip of their island which the English called Land's End was disappearing to the northeast as the *Obong* carved its route on the ocean's green-glass surface and sent tremulous wavelets in a futile pursuit of the land she had left the day before.

He had thought of himself then as akin to Saint Paul on one of his missionary journeys. By sheer force of the will he was going to claim on God's behalf a territory as wide as the ocean itself. A visionary. But had he not superseded his original bargain which was just to become a priest? Wasn't that virtue? Was his move from *contemplation* to *action* not virtue?

Africa had burst upon him, no longer with the romance that was due to distance, no longer with the hazy perception derived from books. This was the real thing. The tropical sun puffed its hellish breath; the steam-chamber atmosphere stifled breathing. The mosquitoes and tsetse flies were real; and so were the half-naked natives. The storms. The darkness. He had brought a faith here, a saving faith. The natives seemed to ask why, and God, by his seeming indifference seemed to ask wherefore – as if on one hand he had not been invited and on the other he had not been sent. For whom then did he work? And to what end?

Rituals on the culprits. Two men were scraping the pubic hair off their genitals. For the first time there was an expression of pain on Philip's face, as the blunt, home-made razor chewed at the tough hair and the skin on which it grew.

Hair from both culprits was put together and set on fire. Everyone turned away symbolically. A tortoise was produced, its back scratched to make it emerge from its shell. It was then beheaded, the shell removed, and the blood dripped over the heads of both Philip and the girl. Then the head was struck over their genitals. Twelve eggs were de-shelled, their mucus was painted over the culprit's organs. More rituals and then everyone fell silent.

Father Higler looked at Philip and tears welled up at the ends of his eyes. But no! This was no time for remorse and self-blame but for action. He had to save Philip, redeem him before man and before God. Redeem himself! But how? What could he do?

Philip's voice startled him as it rang strongly into the night. 'Spare her! Spare her! Spare her! She did not make the choice. I did it to her. I forced her. She has only half a mind! How can she be guilty?'

'His tongue is still loose!'

'Pour some punishment on him!'

'Is not your protection of her rather late?'

'Gag him!'

'Cut off his tongue! In a short time he will not need it.'

'The White Man is trying to speak.'

'No! All speeches are done.'

Father Higler: 'Spare him. Please spare him!'.

'Spare him? He has not committed an offence in your eyes?'

'He has. *This*, and others you don't even know about. But you are the arbiters of his punishment. We have, all of us, committed sin at one time or another.'

'Has anyone else here committed *incest*?'

Father Higler: 'Not incest perhaps, but other things. The just man falls seventy times a day, so it is written. And if the Lord would count iniquities, who among us would be spared?'

'Gibberish, White Man! We cannot default on our obligation and harbour the bad blood.'

'Do you think we like doing it?'

'He has already put a stain on our generation. We cannot add to it by not giving him the punishment he deserves.'

Father Higler: 'Punish him as you will, but spare his life. Release him into my custody. I promise to go away with him and never come back here. Both of us.'

'No!' the old men roared in unison.

'No!' came Philip's solitary but loud protest. 'I do not wish to be spared. This is the end.'

Walking forward towards him, Father Higler asked the servant: Why, Philip, why?'

'I am satisfied now,' Philip replied. 'I have my revenge now. My life is no more use to me. I have no fear to lose it. I will not save it now because I then go back to fear of losing it and running to save it. Here I am, I say. No more running.'

'You are mad, Philip. Quite mad, it is clear to me. And I wish almighty God would grant you one lucid interval, so that I could reach you. What about your eternal salvation? Will you abandon that too as well as your life?'

'Who can guarantee my salvation?'

'God! Almighty God!' Father Higler was now shouting. Tears were raining from his eyes. His hands were thrown out wide, and his head uplifted in the manner of an Old-Law priest at prayer.

The old men, temporarily impressed by the exchange and by the earnestness of the White Man's display, had not yet interfered.

'Philip!' Father Higler yelled.

'Fada.'

'Listen to me, please. Please listen. Be sorry! For what you have done is heinous before both God and man. Make an act of contrition.'

'My sorrows are exhausted too.'

'Enough!' some elder said, then a group of them moved to usher the priest away.

But in one eternal moment, something clicked within him. 'No!' he screamed. 'No!' He saw a machete leaning against a stump, dived for it and whirled around brandishing it. 'No!' he cried. 'You cannot do it!' Philip was yet to be saved. He would save Philip, on his own life.

'Stand away from me, I tell you! And from him! All of you! Do not lay a hand on him.'

The old men backed away in their surprise. The priest backed towards Philip, made a quick turn and cut his bonds loose.

'You are free now, Philip! Run away! Run! Escape!'

Philip did not move but stood and held his hands as if he were still bound.

'You are free, Philip!' Father Higler shouted. 'Go! You are free!'

Just then two old men lunged at the priest in an attempt to wrest the machete from him. Quick as a flash, Philip shoved the priest aside and to the ground, so that both assailants missed him. The servant also came in possession of the machete.

'Now,' Philip said, holding the machete aloft.

A pall fell on the old men, and they bemoaned their younger days when they were stronger and more agile.

'Now,' Philip said again, and waved the machete in their faces.

A few grabbed the other machetes.

'Put them down!' Philip thundered like an angry god. 'Or you wish your head to be the first to roll, or your entrails the first to be poured out!'

'He is mad. Look at his eyes.'

'We should have finished with him sooner.'

'The White Man is to blame for this.'

'He ought to get *it* too.'

'He will.'

'You will get it even before him,' Philip shouted, advancing towards the last speaker. He lifted the machete, and the old man shrieked in fear, guarded his head with his hands. Philip flailed the machete, missing him by scarcely an inch.

'Who among you is not afraid?' Philip asked. 'Who? . . .' He waved the machete wildly, feinting and thrusting, and he rounded them like a sheep dog into an ever-tightening huddle. They ducked as he flailed the machete, cowered, and gasped. Suddenly he was like a god to them, a present and immediate god, vindictive and wrathful, mindless. They were transformed in their fear, speechless. Even Old Man Ahamba, who could pack the universe into a bottle and whose tongue could rattle like summer lightning, was speechless.

Philip set upon the assembly of jujus and began smashing them just as he had done the priest's tabernacle. Uncontrolled frenzy. He whirled, thinking someone was about to jump him. It was Father Higler. The broad machete was lifted over the servant's head and his hand was cocked as if to slice the priest in two.

Father Higler stood his ground, but his breath, his heart, all his senses suspended action. So this was it, was it? the priest was thinking. His mind began reciting an Act of Contrition.

'Fada!' '

'Philip!'

'Go! Go now! Escape! If you wish. No one else needs to die!'

'No one need die at all, Philip,' Father Higler replied, released from his erstwhile fears. 'Think, Philip, think! Before you do anything rash. You and I together, we can find a way out. We can make it to Aba in safety.'

'No. I must die my own death. But if my life has been useless, then my death too. It must be without use.' He waved the machete at the elders. 'Yes, I will die, but I will not die at your hands, like a goat in sacrifice, so that your hearts can stop their trembling and your minds can have peace. Ha-ha. See how I die – at my own hands! . . .'

He suddenly turned the machete on himself, gripped it in both hands and drove the blade through his belly, gasping 'Ah!' as the blood rushed out and he crumpled to the damp ground.

Wide-eyed and open-mouthed, Father Higler raised his hands in the air and then brought them down again beside him hopelessly. Philip in his final throes was beyond help in both body and soul. Father Higler nevertheless pronounced God's mercy on him: '*Miseratur tui omnipotens Deus, et dimissis peccatis tuis, perducat te ad vitam aeternam!*'

The priest crossed himself, and while he had time, as the elders had not yet been released from the spell which events had cast upon them, he broke into the bush and ran.

Old Man Ahamba pushed through the small ring of night fisherman and canoeists that surrounded him. Paused for a moment to regard him as he sat – half sitting, half prostrate – on the dirty sands of the river's bank. The fishers had fished him out, an act which he probably regarded as a dubious favour. He had no shoes. His soutane was shredded, as if the forest through which he had passed had attempted to de-vest him. His underclothes, too, were torn, and so was his skin marked with dozens of bruises and scratches, the blood on them caked, softened by his immersion in the water, then caked again.

His eyes moved for the first time in reaction to the pair of feet – Ahamba's – which were planted in the sand hardly a yard from him. His head began to lift. His eyes climbed the legs – up, up, up, to the face of their owner. Ahamba extended a hand and hoisted him up. He tried his legs like a young animal learning to walk.

'Come,' Ahamba said, leading him by the hand to the water's edge. 'Kneel!' Taking him by the scruff of the neck, Ahamba immersed his head three times in the dirty foot waters of the river, re-baptizing him. 'Take a drink of it if you like . . . Ah yes, everything is now restored, just as it was. Except for the scars. You have now arrived. How many years are you? . . . This is not the end, though, only a halfway point, a stop in the middle of the road, though some mistake it for the final destination and never go beyond it. But you must go beyond it. Stand. Come . . .'

They moved from the edge of the water. 'But did you hear him?'
'Who?'
'Your pot boiler.'

He exhaled. 'God, almighty God! . . . He did not know what he was doing.'

'It would be nice if the gods sometimes let us know what they were doing.'

'He was crazy! Insane!'

'He found the truth and it drove him to despair. Even to madness as you say. He did what he did in despair. The truth is dangerous.'

'Of what truth do you now speak?'

'The secret which makes us human and keeps the gods divine to us. Few men ever find the truth and survive it. It is a dangerous secret. The trick is to take as much truth as we can bear and go on living . . . What will you do now?'

'What are my choices?'

'My friend, you make them yourself.'

His head ached. His entire body ached. His mind refused to engage any thoughts. He lifted his eyes to the horizon where the gilded edge of the sky touched the dark green top of the forest. Joining hands, sky and land were swaying to and fro like two dancers, humming: 'We are gods together! We are gods together . . .'